❧

PARIS, 1933:

Written as a lost volume from her celebrated diaries, ANAÏS NIN AT THE GRAND GUIGNOL *follows the iconic feminist author into an erotic and twilit realm of dark fantasy and sexual obsession, a world of forbidden desire and deadly consequence from which she might never fully return.*

In the aftermath of her love triangle with novelist HENRY MILLER and his dancer wife June, thirty-year-old ANAÏS NIN is left reeling. Stifled by her bourgeois marriage, she retreats into the midnight world of the GRAND GUIGNOL, the legendary theatre of horror and fear whose devoted patrons thrill at the macabre spectacles depicted on the black box stage. It is there that she falls under the spell of the actress PAULA MAXA, known as THE MOST MURDERED WOMAN OF ALL TIME, who awakens Anaïs to a secret realm of bewitchment and vice, of pleasure and pain.

Only Maxa already belongs to MONSIEUR GUILLARD, the lustful night creature that haunts the dark streets of Pigalle. As the demon lover's insatiable hunger grows stronger by the hour, Anaïs finds herself trapped in a far more dangerous triangle, a cat-and-mouse game with Maxa's very soul as the ultimate prize.

❧

ANAÏS NIN at The GRAND GUIGNOL

ROBERT LEVY

LETHE PRESS
AMHERST, MA

Published by Lᴇᴛʜᴇ Pʀᴇss
lethepressbooks.com

Copyright © 2019 Robert Levy

ISBN: 978159021717

Library of Congress Cataloging-in-Publication Data
available on request

Cover and Interior design by Iɴᴋsᴘɪʀᴀʟ Dᴇsɪɢɴ

Cover art adapted from
Tʜᴇ Dᴀɴᴄᴇ ᴏꜰ Dᴇᴀᴛʜ (Tᴏᴛᴇɴᴛᴀɴᴢ)

For

Dr. Louise Bordeaux Silverstein,
who first showed me the diaries

and

Mel Gordon,
who showed us the way
to 20bis Rue Chaptal

"Before I go to bed, I look under my bed with fear. I fear the dark, the storms, the sea, the unknown and my own darkness."

PAULA MAXA

PARIS

1933

While Hugo is in London, Henry comes to see me at Louveciennes. Emilia serves us a lovely lunch of steamed clams and a salade niçoise, as well as the festive carrot soufflé from my aunt's recipe, all of which Henry takes to with his usual lustful brio. He drinks and I smoke, and we play with the dogs in the garden while we wait for Emilia to clear away the dishes. I watch as Henry tosses the ball out for Banquo, who brings it back for another go, just one more, one more, more. I retain a smile, but this surface contentment is an inaccurate reflection of what lies beneath, a mask I wear so that I might be found respectable and worthy of companionship. In truth, I am adrift.

I give Emilia the afternoon off and send her home early. No sooner is she out and past the green garden gate than Henry and I set upon each other, hungry and wild, and we caress with an unmoored enthusiasm.

"How long do we have?" he says, as we make our way up the stairs. "Tell me I can stay the night."

"Another night, but not this one. I have too many errands to tend to in advance of Hugo's return. Then he is back here through the end of April."

"Damn it to hell. I did hear somewhere that April was the cruelest month." Henry hikes my dress up and around my waist. "'Breeding lilacs out of the dead land...'"

"'Mixing memory and desire, stirring dull roots with spring rain....'"

"Hey, you know your Waste Land," he says, and he presses himself against me, no time to disrobe before I feel him hard against my thigh. "I'm impressed."

"I know a great many things besides Eliot." I smile, with a wicked knowledge born of experience. "Allow me to show them to you."

I move toward the bed, but "No," he whispers in my ear, "right here," and he takes hold of my buttocks in his rough tailor's hands and seats me upon the windowsill.

I fumble with his belt buckle, release him from the confines of his trousers and worn-out underwear. I help him from the remainder of his clothing, as he helps me from mine, our costumes shed so that we may be free from the staged production of our ordinary lives. We cross over as one into the more real world of fantasy, undiminished and undisguised, my native country above all others. For it is only in the act of pleasure that I can find myself, my true self. There, and in this diary.

Henry thrusts himself inside me, and the whole of my body spasms, his iron embrace all that keeps me from crashing through the leaded glass at my back. I grasp him closer, tilt my pelvis so that the small core at my opening bears down upon his firmness. I squeeze my eyes shut and ride him faster, my panting breath unfurling into a quiet and steady prayer.

"Please," I whisper, "please," not so much to Henry as to a distant god of mercy. This is the only way I know how to heal what has been broken.

"Oh, Christ, Anaïs," he mutters, and I scramble for leverage against the walls of the window casing, fingernails scarring the plaster with crescent-shaped marks, lest they find a softer target and draw blood.

"You make me crazy," he says. "There's no one else but you. You know that. There's no one else in the world." The animal sounds of our lovemaking echo in my ears, ring out across the bedroom and through the open door, and we fall into a dance of wordlessness, into the language of movement, the divine alchemy of the physical.

The wordlessness is just as well, since I cannot respond to Henry in kind. I cannot tell him there is no one else, because unlike him I am not so quick to lie. I know he believes these words as he speaks them, however, just as I know that, in another moment or five moments or ten, his imagination will steer toward one of his many whores. Or perhaps toward June, glittering and regal and imperious. The billowing curves of her hips and breasts, her severe face that captures the female and the male in its own golden ratio, she who commands the beauty of both sexes at once. Since she left for New York, a whirlpool of loss has opened inside me, one capable of swallowing me whole. My longing for her is so powerful it disturbs me.

As Henry spends himself inside me, I wonder if he thinks of her now, and the affair that sent her away. The one that Henry and I have carried on for all these many months, that drove his wife from his arms. I wonder because I cannot help but think of June myself.

∾

I GO INTO the city for my session with Dr. Allendy. The small office he keeps at his home address is uncomfortably warm, a strange humidity laced with pipe smoke that narcotizes me as soon as I enter.

"Close your eyes," he says. "Relax, and simply talk." I lie upon the couch, and he steers me down the usual paths of analysis: my dissatisfactions with domesticity and my role as a wife; the highs and inevitable lows brought on by my various love affairs; the loss of June, and what it means for both Henry and myself. As the session progresses, I find myself unable to concentrate on the task at hand, to draw upon the usual connections and associations crucial to therapeutic success. Somewhere along the dance of my life, I have lost my footing, and I can no longer disguise it when I drop a step.

"Anaïs? What is the matter?" Allendy strokes his beard as he stares down at me with his typical air of avuncular concern. "You do not seem quite yourself today."

"It is nothing," I say, though neither of us is fooled by these empty words. "It is just..." I shake my head. "I am beginning to feel I am not present in my own life. That I have taken on the role of an observer. It is as if I am somehow outside of my skin, cursed to look on as I go about my daily business. I worry that I am becoming a stranger to myself."

"Perhaps this sense of separation is due to your work," Allendy says. "Is it not possible that this secondary life on the page—your mirror life—is actually subsuming your everyday existence? Nowhere is this more acute than in the case of your obsessive diary writing." I feel my journal from the corner of the room, where it burns inside my bag like a fiery cinder, an irrepressible itch in need of scratching. It begs to be written inside of, page after page and cover to cover. I am an addict, it is true, the diary no less than my opium.

"Normally, I would be inclined to agree," I say. "But it is not my writing that has caused me to feel this way. It is as if I have become my own ghost."

"Do you have any thoughts about what might be causing this sense of dissociation?" Allendy crosses and uncrosses his legs, brings his pipe to his mouth. I exhale, and contemplate how best to answer.

"You want me to say it is because of June," I say. "It is true that wanted to save her from the pallid existence she had made for herself, and the ruins of her marriage to Henry. But June is the death drive that counterbalances Henry's vitality, his love of life. And now? Now, she is gone. Her choice, of course. She proved once and for all that she did not desire saving in the first place. Least of all by me."

"Then perhaps it is time for you to find someone else on which to focus." He bites at the lip of his pipe before slipping it from his mouth. "Perhaps it is time for you find someone else to save."

"Perhaps it is."

I stare out the window, at the tops of the honey locust trees in Allendy's garden, their flowers just beginning to blossom on the far side of the glass. "At Louveciennes," I say, "behind the wide wooden trellis covered in thick ivy, the front of the house is faced with shutters. There are eleven of them: five windows onto the west rooms, and five onto the east, with a single closed shutter at its center. That center shutter is always closed, you see, because it is only there for symmetry. There is nothing behind it, no window or room whatsoever. Yet I often find myself dreaming that there is in fact a room, a place I call the sealed room. I imagine that if only I can locate the door and manage to unlock it, then what lies inside will prove the missing element that is destined to complete me at last."

"This sealed room," Allendy says. "It is where your unknown self is kept from you, yes? Your own private mysteries, hidden away. The essence of your repressed desires."

I nod. "And so I am unmoored, and doomed to continue searching for what I have lost, the way I search for the room in my dreams. Unmoored more than usual, it must be said, in June's wake."

"Yet she is not the primal cause of your malaise." Allendy taps out his pipe in the ashtray, though his dark eyes remain fixed upon me, pinning me to the couch like a specimen. "Your feelings about her absence are but an echo of the original and formative event: the abandonment you suffered at the hands your father."

"Maybe so," I say, and shift uncomfortably upon the couch, the room growing hotter. "I feel betrayed by her. An echo of the loss, as you say, that I felt as a child. The difference, however, is that June left because of Henry and me. She claimed I was the source of the entire rupture."

"You said Henry and June's marriage was foundering long before they moved to Paris and crossed your path. In truth, your guilt is precisely the same self-blame you bore in the aftermath of your father's abandonment. It stems from your unconscious conviction that if only you had managed to be a better daughter, then your father would never have left."

He smiles. "This desire for self-flagellation is a knot at the center of your resistant mind, Anaïs, one that is in desperate need of untying. Your shame is also the cause of your masochistic dreams, those in which you desire to be dominated. Indeed, to be punished, humiliated. Your intense desire for your father's affections is coupled with your allegiance to your betrayed mother, aligned as you are with her sense of outrage. You find it easy to place yourself in her position, that of an abandoned lover, yes? This naturally lends itself to feelings of inadequacy. Have you had any erotic dreams about your father?"

I smooth my dress over my knees, and look up to find him watching me. "How do you suggest I free myself from this cycle of self-punishment?"

He puts down his pipe and stands. "I want to show you something."

I follow him out of his office and into the adjoining parlor. Against the far wall is a square slatted box the size of a wardrobe, the dark brown wood out of place amid the room's black-and-white decor.

"This is called an isolation accumulator." He opens the door to the structure to reveal its metal interior. "It is a prototype created by a former colleague at the Vienna Ambulatorium, designed to stimulate the production of positive flow through the lessening of distractibility. I would like you to try it, to better open yourself to that which keeps you from healthful integration."

"And…how do I go about using it, exactly?"

"You sit inside, and I shut the door." Allendy slides a chair from the nearby table and places it in the box. "Then, you close your eyes, and you breathe. Consider your feelings of guilt and shame, and how these repressive emotions are ultimately of your own making. Picture them as particles of negativity among a sea of energy, energy that you are able to disperse, until you are awash in positive light alone."

Allendy steps away from the box. "I will open

the door in twenty minutes, with time to share and evaluate your experience. That is all you have to do."

I enter the small chamber and settle into the chair, and he swings the door closed. I am sealed inside, with only the darkness as my companion. At first, the totality of silence is unnerving. There is a dull throbbing in my ears, though I soon recognize it as the sound of my heart beating, the blood as it pumps through my veins.

I begin to relax into my seat. My mind wanders, and my thoughts drift from Allendy to my husband, from Hugo to Henry to June, a rotating cast of characters whose features blur together until I am faced with a single mask-like face. Or perhaps it is a mixture of faces, the skin there smooth and colorless and without any discernible attributes, unformed as a lump of clay. I attempt to shape the features into those of my father, but I find a stubborn resistance there, an unwillingness to summon him from the ether of my imagination.

The smell of the sea, the touch of silt and sand and rock beneath my toes, and I am naked and stretched out upon a strangely familiar shore. The seaside of my youth in New York, perhaps, or maybe Cuba, I cannot say for certain. The waves make a gentle slapping sound, and a lone gull wheels overhead. The sun is low to the earth, a swollen and bloody ball in the process of sinking beneath the horizon. *Red sky at night, sailor's delight*. The words taught to me by my father, just before he left us for good.

How I prayed to God that he would return to me, that he would love me and possess me completely. The way a devoted husband loves a wife, with every fiber of his being. God never answered, however, and so I stopped praying. I began the diary instead.

I sit up inside my reverie, and shield my eyes from the harsh glare. There is someone in the water, up to his or her neck and backlit by the blurred red orb of sun that hovers over the ocean like a glutted leech. Silver-yellow eyes gleam from their skull, twin flames flickering as they watch from the waves.

The figure wades toward me, toward the shore, and now I can see that it is a man. He is tall and broad-shouldered, his face obscured as he approaches. At once, the sky blackens and a storm front rolls over the beach, angry clouds blotting out the sun and plunging the world into darkness. The tide rushes across the shore to drench my limbs, and a furious wind whips my hair about me, a conjured chaos descending everywhere at once as I stand and begin to run.

A talon grip takes hold of my ankle and pulls me to the ground. A human hand, yet unlike any I have ever seen or felt, its strength icy and elemental. I struggle to free myself, my fingers raking across sand and rock. It is no use, however, and I am dragged back across the remainder of the shore and into the sea's cold embrace. The weight of the ocean bears down upon me, saltwater stinging my eyes, my throat, filling my lungs with its unyielding pressure, and as I drown I attempt to scream.

I know that I must rouse myself from this waking nightmare. And yet a strange comfort passes over me, a dark knowledge that it will all be over soon, if only I surrender to it. I must fight this impulse as well.

I flail my arms, my palms smacking against smooth walls on either side of me, and I am back inside the strange box in Allendy's office. Only the box is filled to the brim with seawater, and I am drowning here as well, still caught in the ocean's relentless whirlpool. And all the while, the cold hand grasps my ankle, fingers stroking my calf and lengthening and extending like a tangle of hungry eels to coil about my thigh. A slender and viscous digit finds its way up and inside me, filling me as the brine fills my eyes and mouth, my ears and nose. I am consumed.

A brightness flares in the dark, and I wince. Allendy stands before me, framed in the entry to the slatted box, the light of day animating motes of dust winking in the air around him. I leap up and hurry from the box, my hands clamped to my arms to keep from trembling as I move past him and down the hall.

"Anaïs?" Allendy calls after me. "Are you all right? You cried out."

"So sorry, doctor, but I forgot that I am due at home earlier than usual." I calm my breath as I meet his watchful eyes. "We will continue this next week, yes?"

"Of course," he says, his expression tightening with unspoken concern. "We will pick up where we left off."

I thank him and head out onto Rue de l'Assomption. As I glance over my shoulder, I notice for the first time the resemblance between Allendy's quaint townhouse and the house where we lived in Brussels when I was a child. How the whole of my existence becomes a vast echo over time and space, from which there is never any escape. I shake away the observation, just as I negate the conjured image of the predatory yellow eyes staring out from the dark ocean's unsettled waters.

I continue down the street, and give myself over to the dirty swirl of the city, allow its anonymous embrace to erase my panicked state. Still, the fear refuses to let me go. I conjured a horrible fate inside the box, it is true, one of a mysterious and unearthly creature drowning me, penetrating me, more. Another manifested daydream of submission, as Allendy would surely have noted if I had summoned the courage to reveal this disturbing product of my fragmented imagination.

My dark desires, they have long carried a vast and primitive voluptuousness capable of opening doors between places I once thought locked forever, a rising tide of sensual oblivion I had hoped to bury for good. Forbidden pleasures rooted in taboo desire, transmuted by my imagination in much the same way I transform my intimacies into art. And who can say for certain where it is these desires might take me? Perhaps I will discover the door to my sealed room after all.

∾

HUGO HAS RETURNED from his business trip. Following dinner, we retire to the living room, where we sit in front of the hearth. He is hard at work on his latest hobby, a detailed series of astrology charts, while I write in my diary, the dogs curled up together on the floor between us. After some time, I look up to find Hugo watching me, and any sense of focus or resolve dissipates like the early morning fog over the village. His gaze is soft, but it penetrates nevertheless.

"What is it?" I ask. "Is there something the matter?"

"I was just thinking how very lucky I am," he says. "Not only to have a wife of such exquisite beauty, but one so devoted to her art. You are in every way an inspiration to me."

I laugh, and the effort feels false, an attempt to conceal an essential dissatisfaction behind a veil of mirth. "If I am able to brighten your mood in this way, and after all this time," I say, "then I shall consider it an accomplishment. You know how important my writing is to me, that I cannot live in the real world alone. As for your admiration of my appearance, that says more about the kindness of your eye that it does about my looks. Paris has many ladies who are far more alluring."

"You do yourself an injustice, Anaïs. You are the most ravishing woman I know."

"All this?" I gesture with lacquered nails at my painted face, my silk dressing gown. "It is but an illusion. Feminine inventiveness, if you will. As for my art, well..." I smooth the pulped pages of my journal. "I believe in myself, and what I do. But as there are greater beauties, there are greater writers as well. Important ones, whose work will one day change the world."

"Like Henry." The hint of betrayal is plain in Hugo's voice. It is a strange relief to hear Henry's name, since in a sense he was already here with us, a vaporous phantom lingering smoke-like between us. It is to Hugo's great credit that he can acknowledge my needs outside our union, that in his own quiet way he allows me the freedoms I find necessary to live a life of bohemianism, of excitement. But what good can come of these liaisons, when the anguish they inevitably yield proves as robust as the passion itself?

"You know how much I respect Henry's dedication and talent," I say. "I have no need to compare myself to him. Not when there is so much more for us both to accomplish."

"You have great faith in him."

"I do." I close the cover of my diary, press it hard

to my chest like a holy object. "I understand Henry on that level, and he understands me in the same manner. We recognize the artist in each other, and see ourselves for what we are."

"He may see the artist inside you, but I see the woman." Hugo kneels beside my chair, his spectacles catching the amber light from the fire. "Let us do something special together this evening. Something gay, just the two of us."

"Wouldn't you prefer to spend the evening at home?" I cup his eager face in my hands. "You have been gone the better part of a week."

"First a night out, and then the whole of the day tomorrow lazing in bed. I want to show you off to the world."

We kiss, tenderly. "How can I refuse such flattery?"

"Wonderful. So. Where is it you would most like to go?"

I inhale, and, in an instant, I find myself startled to return to a certain cold December night. It was my first outing with June, not so very long ago but still part of some other era, another age. Dinner at Louveciennes, and then a car into the city to the theatre. Hugo and

Henry discussed politics, while June and I nestled together in the back, huddled close and whispering shared secrets like schoolgirls. When we reached the theatre, she extended her hand, beckoning me from the car like a siren to my own shipwreck.

I knew in that moment that I would do anything she asked. That perhaps I always would, no matter where her destructive spirit took me. She is Thanatos, braided through Eros in a tightly knotted rope.

How appropriate, then, that we had decided that evening to visit the holy palace of such matters. That night in the theatre, I was so taken with her I had barely paid attention to the show. Seated between her and Hugo, it was only June that I watched out of the corner of my eye. Her face contorted in skeptical bemusement as ghastly scenarios of bloodletting and torture unfolded before us, only to roll her eyes once the act ended and shifted into the next. Even in my state of distraction, I laughed and cried out in revulsion along with the rest of the audience, swept away in a tide of emotion that June seemed unable to access. My heart near bursting with feeling, with a rapidly unfolding desire for her that was so overwhelming it threatened to engulf the world. In that perverse theatre and under the cover of its luxuriant darkness, I had felt more alive than ever.

"Darling man." I smile at Hugo, and take his hands in mine. "I want to go to the Grand Guignol."

∾

I STAND IN front of the theatre and smoke as Hugo waits on line at the box office to retrieve our tickets. The dark and narrow street outside 20bis Rue Chaptal is bustling, the cobbled court glutted with preening couples, high-heeled women on the arms of their companions to steady them as they negotiate the uneven stones. The Theatre du Grand-Guignol is nothing if not an ideal night out for the amorous, lovers who innocently enter the small Pigalle black box only to cling to each other in paroxysms of laughter or fright, the emotionally heightened scenarios blossoming like poisonous flowers upon the stage.

"Shall we go inside?" Hugo says, returned to my side.

We file through the heavy oak doors alongside the other patrons, traverse the crowded foyer and stop at the bar for a drink. As we enter the theatre proper, we are handed our programs, and I inhale the room's heady and contradictory scents, what

Tulsa City-County Library

Hardesty Regional Library

To Renew: www.tulsalibrary.org

918-549-7323

Date: 5/17/2024

Time: 1:31:44 PM

Fines/Fees Owed: $0.00

Total Checked Out This Session: 1

Checked Out

Title: Spaced out : how the NBA's three-point revolution changed everything you thought you knew about bask
Barcode: 32345092617191
Due Date: 05-31-24 (*)

Thank you for visiting the library!

D.H. Lawrence might refer to as *fug*: perfume and cigarette smoke, must and alcohol, greasepaint and dry ice. The building was once a chapel, and the space still carries something of the sacred, tapestries hung from the baroque wood paneling and arched beams decorated with carved gods and monsters, angels and demons, the vaulted ceiling thatched with fleur-de-lis and pierced by iron chandeliers. Special patrons watch the performances from the row of confessional boxes at the rear of the theatre, where the amorous are free to hide behind ornate mesh screens and carry on their dalliances unseen.

We pass beneath the balcony's low overhang, make our way to our seats in the pew-like rows at the middle of the house. We wait, and soon the lights dim, as a backstage accordionist squeezes out a jaunty tune upon a weathered concertina. A portly master of ceremonies appears in front of the red velvet curtain. He is dressed in formal evening wear, top hat and all, though the attire is shabby, a worn pose from the hazy past. He walks the half-dozen steps to the foot of the small stage, where he clears his throat, rocking on his scuffed heels until the accordionist ceases to play.

"Ladies and gentlemen," he says with great portent,

"thank you for joining us this evening in the bastion of pleasure and terror, virtue and vice. Tonight, your most hidden desires and private fears will be conjured upon our humble stage, so that you may delight and despair in the darkest corners of your imagination. Welcome to the Grand Guignol!"

A renewed squeal of song, and the curtain rises upon a pastoral scene, a busty shepherdess standing in front of a backdrop depicting an alpine idyll of rolling hills beneath a bright blue sky. She wears a traditional taffeta dress and bears an oversized crook, and she glides across the stage while singing a sprightly little song, an echo of the accordionist's opening number.

"Oh, how lonely is the life of a shepherdess," she bemoans in a girlish falsetto, a lace-gloved hand pressed to her brow. "If only I had a handsome man with me as I tend to my flock."

A broad-shouldered herder in lederhosen and a feathered cap enters to boisterous appreciation from the audience. "Oh, how lonely is the life of a goat herder," he calls out. "If only I had a fair maiden for company as I see to my goats."

Hugo strokes my hand, and he smiles over at me, a smile I am only too happy to return. He laughs when

I laugh, I whistle when he whistles, the both of us taking care to ensure the other is enjoying themselves, engaging in the playful camaraderie that Henry disparagingly calls our love antics. But inside me, the swirling question makes itself known, the one that says:

How can you pretend to be fulfilled, Anaïs, when the aching emptiness still lurks inside you? The void that took shape when you were a young girl and first drank of the deep well of loneliness, it remains, and will stay with you until your life is finally over. Only then will the pain cease at last.

I twist in my seat, as if upon an instrument of slow torture.

Not three minutes pass before the goat herder has the shepherdess stripped to her undergarments. He thrusts himself upon her, their interlocking bodies only somewhat obscured by stuffed goats and sheep rolled in by stagehands on poorly disguised casters, tufts of cotton and fur billowing out into the pews as the audience hollers and cheers their approval. This is the light, before the darkness takes over.

I allow myself to fall into the familiar rhythm of the Guignol. The ludicrous machinations of the sex farce giving way to the degradations of a *rosse* play depicting a cruel soldier as he menaces a negligee-clad prostitute, and then a return to broad comedy again, the jarring dissonance leaving the audience delirious and hungry for more. It is the theatre's signature method of alternating between extremes, the acts vacillating so that we are taken from hilarity to terror, from sexual libertinism to sexualized violence. The audience is provided with the effect of *une douche écossaise*, and indeed I blush with the force of each novel sensation, blood rushing to the surface of my newly awakened skin.

After a brief interval, the curtain opens once more, onto an ominous and candlelit stage. The scene is that of an off-kilter hospital, the sharp angles of the spare black-and-white set pieces jutting out at irregular angles akin to a small-scale reproduction of *The Cabinet of Dr. Caligari*. An operating table and surgical stand are positioned at center stage, and a murmur of appreciation passes over the crowd. This is what we came for.

Two uniformed attendants enter with a straightjacketed woman between them, the patient struggling against her restraints to no avail. They strap her down screaming upon the table, her hair a nest of unkempt blond curls, face gaunt with bulging and haunted eyes. In the flickering candlelight, she is odd-looking, but in her own way she is beautiful, with an air of the familiar. I suspect I may have seen her before.

A moment later a doctor emerges from the wings. Balding and extremely thin, he appears almost skeletal beneath his white apron and surgical clothes. "I see the nymphomania treatments have failed to yield the desired results," he says over her cries, his tone disturbingly cool. "I will have to take more drastic measures to relieve our patient of her unquenchable cravings. Thank you, gentlemen, that will be all. I shall call for you again once the procedure is complete."

The aides depart, and the doctor bends over the patient's supine form. His hands roam her body, undoing the laces of her straightjacket and reaching inside the loose cotton nightgown beneath. He frees her breasts, which are fuller and less firm than my own, and he squeezes one of them, pinches the large brown nipple so that it hardens like a raisin. The woman stifles a cry, her eyes widening into round white circles. I am transfixed.

"You've given us all a great deal of trouble, Christine." The doctor plucks a scalpel from the tray upon the surgical stand. "But now it is time for us to bring a halt to the hysteria, for your tragic condition to come to an end. It is time for you to find your relief at last."

He brings the knife to the edge of her nipple and begins to cut into her flesh. She shrieks with wild intensity, bucking against the leather straps that bind her to the table. Blood trickles fast from her breast, her alabaster skin running red in a dark wet current. Stagecraft, yes, but with the illusion of sickening realism all the same. Hugo and I squeeze each other's hands as the patient's agonized face shifts in the candle flame. Beneath her powder and paint, past a damp sweep of tangled hair draped across her brow, the bloodied victim wears a new face. June's face.

I gasp. A woman screams behind me, just as the stage lights blare brightly in unsettling patches of green and yellow. I dare not take my eyes from the stage, from the bleeding patient and her tortured expression, June's eyes pleading for release from her perdition. As the blood-soaked nipple is sliced away and delivered as a delicacy to the doctor's eager lips, all I can see is that it is June who is defiled. In this conjured vision of her degradation upon the stage, I feel only abandon, for the first time in far too long. In a most unexpected way, I feel alive again.

The doctor chews the nipple with noticeable relish, and the audience roars in disgusted horror, the balcony loudest of all, with the greatest vantage point of this particular carnage. The maniac physician swallows and laughs and sets to work on the other nipple, severing the brown tip with great gusto. A man rises from a nearby seat and stumbles into the aisle, where he falls in a dead faint, an usher rushing to assist him.

With a final cry of terror, June's body slackens, and her head lolls to the side. For one brief moment our gazes lock, until her eyes close and the actress succumbs to a feigned unconsciousness.

"Now, my tender and delicious Christine," the doctor says, "let us see what you have down between your legs, shall we?" He lowers the scalpel, and the crowd shrieks as the curtain comes down, Hugo squirming next to me as we applaud the sordid play's appalling conclusion.

I bring his hand to my lips and kiss his knuckles, the room electrified with murmurs and movement as the patrons resettle in their seats. Like me, they are unsure how to feel, how best to absorb and respond to what has just taken place before them. Did they see their own objects of desire and longing in the patient, the way that I saw June? Did it make them feel the same exquisite satisfaction, the first twinge of a new and awakening pleasure inside?

The curtain rises upon another ribald comedy. The audience laughs and whistles, Hugo along with them, lulled into another scene of bawdy seduction and innuendo. Yet I am somewhere else now, inside my head. I am back in the operating room, the fiend standing above June as he grasps her breast in one hand and the scalpel in the other, a seam of yellow candlelight gleaming from the blade.

I hunch over in the pew, and in the dark I seek out the soft pebble of one of my nipples. I pinch it until it stiffens, so hard that I am afraid it will burst.

At intermission, Hugo and I hang on each other as if we are drunk. Once we exit the theatre, he immediately leads me through the crowd and raises his hand to flag down a taxi. "The show is not yet over," I say as he opens the door for me, but it does nothing to dissuade him. He need not say why, the lust plain on his face. I recognize it for what it is, almost as well as I am capable of recognizing my own. He provides the driver with directions, and the moment the car pulls away from the theatre he is upon me. His tongue in my mouth, teeth tugging at my earlobe, lips sucking at my neck until he lowers himself onto the floor of the car, his head foraging between my legs.

"Hugo!" I whisper, startled as he slides my underwear down to my ankles. Though a passionate lover, I have never known him to give himself over to such public and impulsive displays, not in all our many years of marriage. He kisses at my thighs, his enthusiastic tongue wriggling inside me, and I tremble and hold tight to the seat's hard and cracked leather.

As I roll my head back in pleasure, I catch the driver's gaze in the rearview mirror. He watches us, watches me with silver-yellow eyes: it is the stare of a carnivorous beast, malevolent and ravenous. It is the animal gaze of the creature from Allendy's box, a macabre fragment I unwittingly carry inside me as a jagged splinter beneath my skin.

Flush with fear and desire, I begin to moan. I force a knuckle into my mouth, squeeze my eyes shut as I shudder and thrill, Hugo's tongue and lips seeking out the softest and most tender parts of me. With a suppressed cry of joy, I convulse as the car rumbles through the cool Paris night, street lamps streaking past in molten waves as we are delivered back to Louveciennes.

Once we are home, Hugo possesses me completely, his ardor undiminished. I wince as he enters me, and this time I find that I welcome the pain of his penetration. Pain, mixed with pleasure, and I think of the actress on the operating table. The way I had imagined June into the scenario as well, the same way a child daydreams those closest to them as figures in a puppet show, in order to make meaning of a world beyond control. The woman's pleading eyes, her face both June's face and not, commingled by some strange trick of the light. I see her as my husband thrusts inside me. Her and the leering eyes in the taxi's rearview mirror that watched me with such hunger, a demoniac lust that helps quiet the seething void within.

I close my legs about Hugo and bite down on my lip until I begin to draw blood.

∽

I MEET HENRY in the afternoon. We have his flat to ourselves, and we write at the kitchen table and comment on the other's pages, discuss Joyce and Lawrence and Dostoevsky until we are breathless. How pleasant it is to work across from each other at our respective typewriters! Eventually, however, he takes the opportunity of our close proximity to place his hand beneath the table and between my stockinged legs.

"Please, Henry, I am trying to work," I say, and brush his hand away.

"What if we just have a little quickie?" He lowers his glasses down his nose and delivers one of his pleading looks. "Hey, I gotta at least ask, okay? Don't fault me for asking. A man has his needs, after all. You might not understand that, but it's true."

"A man has his needs, but not a woman?" I scowl and cross my arms. "You seem to have forgotten the rest of your Eliot, Mr. Miller. Or at least the source mythology for his poem. Remember the hermaphrodite Tiresias, who was cursed by Hera? And why? For revealing that it is in fact woman, not man, who is the more sensual creature."

"Screw Tiresias," Henry says. "And screw Eliot too. I never liked that guy anyway. So. Maybe just a little hanky-panky after we write a couple more pages?"

"I said no." I make a face, though I cannot help but laugh at his persistence. "That is not what I need from you right now. I need your insight, your raw intellect.

Today, I require a different aspect of your potency. I need the attention of your brain, and not your... prick," I say, borrowing one of his favorite words, and now Henry is the one laughing. "Although if I change my mind, I promise you will be the first to know."

"Can't argue with that. You're the boss, after all." He slides up his glasses with a thick finger and returns his gaze to his typewriter. "But don't think I haven't noticed you've lost a little bit of your swing as of late." By which he means since June left.

"Yes, well, so have you. As of late." I begin to type again, and soon enough he does the same. We fall into a familiar, if not altogether comfortable, silence.

For while it is Henry at Louveciennes who plays the role of the invisible specter that hovers between Hugo and myself, here in Clichy we are haunted by June, who has written Henry to announce that she will not be returning to Paris. He has taken his own childish revenge by removing her picture from the wall and replacing it with one of his lovers, a beautiful dancer from the Bal Nègre. Too complicated to unravel our cat's cradle of affections and recriminations, our seductions and our passions and our hurts, though Henry and I are united by more than our fucking (another of his favorite words).

I jolt anew at June's rage when she discovered our affair, her drunken and tearful declarations of betrayal that evening in their flat made all the more painful because I was not just another one of his nameless dalliances. She must despise the very thought of me, if only because she misconstrued the unspoken arrangement in which we all found ourselves. June and I shared our own voluptuous fantasy, of course, our own distinct form of intimacy. I wonder if I will ever manage to find that same closeness again.

After a lunch of sandwiches at Café de la Place Clichy, I leave Henry to browse the shops, the first perfume blush of spring washing over the city in a tide of pink and yellow and green. I wander aimlessly as if ensorcelled, until it dawns on me that I am traveling in a specific direction, one that soon becomes clear the farther I stroll. Eventually, I must admit to myself where I am headed, and find myself drifting up the narrow street that opens onto Rue Chaptal and the Theatre du Grand-Guignol.

A lone woman, small and dark-haired, stands smoking in front of the shuttered entrance. It is only once I get close enough that I realize it is the actress from Friday evening. In the light of day, she looks nothing like June, and must have been wearing a blond wig as she lay captive and mutilated upon the mad doctor's operating table. Reflexively, my nipples begin to tingle, the mere sight of her enough to trigger a commingled sensation of pleasure and pain. I do not want her to catch me staring, and so I lower my head as I move to cross the street.

"You," the actress calls out. She steps from the shelter of the entryway, her brown eyes searching my face. She appears roughly my age, a few years older perhaps, her face less full without the benefit of stage lighting and theatrical makeup. "You were in the audience here this past weekend."

"What? Oh. Yes. I was." Apropos of nothing, I giggle like a fool, my cheeks flushing. "I enjoyed it very much. The hospital play especially. It was quite disturbing. Gruesome, even. The depravity of the doctor's cannibalism was astounding."

"That?" she scoffs. "That was nothing. A common and sensationalist trifle at best." She lights another cigarette from her last and flicks the spent stub into the gutter. "It is only when we are able to draw from hidden wells of fear that true fright is made known.

Your first time at the Guignol, I take it?"

"Far from it." June beside me in the pew, her bare arm pressed against mine, the dual scents of her perfume and natural musky odor intoxicating. Delirium, darkness, delirium anew. "The Guignol is always a special experience, no matter how often I attend."

"Then you have seen your fair share of horrors. What is cannibalism, then, when compared to uncontrollable lust? Or compared to wanton betrayal? Next to that, eating human flesh is nothing." She exhales in a scattered burst of smoke. "My name is Paula," she says, "but everyone calls me Maxa. Also known as The Maddest Woman in the World. If you've been to the Guignol before, then you've also seen your fair share of me."

"I am sure that I have. Only this was the first time that I..." I shake my head and glance at a poster on the theatre's façade, its image that of a lingerie-clad woman on her knees as she cradles a man's severed head, a coy smile stretched across her blood-red lips.

"Tell me." Maxa's eyes narrow, intrigued and wary in equal measure. "Go on."

I search for the proper words. "It was the first time I found my own story intermingled with that of the proceedings. I saw a friend of mine, violated upon the stage during the hospital scene. I saw her, in your face."

She smiles. "To many patrons, the Guignol functions as a mirror onto their secret desires. *I* function as a mirror, especially for women of a peculiar disposition. The passionate. The artistic. The... conflicted." A coil of smoke slithers out from between her lips. "And how did it make you feel, then, to look upon your friend in such a horrifying predicament? To see her violated like that. Used as chattel is used, treated as if she were but a plaything for a madman. Such demonstrations of sadism and perversion, did they cause you to realize they are mere reflections of what is already inside of you?"

"Yes. Yes, they did." My throat goes dry, and I swallow. A wave of displacement overtakes me, as if I should be back in Allendy's office, answering these invasive questions upon his couch. Only I find that it is here and with this bold actress that I can fully answer from my heart. "It also made me... excited. And it made me feel wholly alive, for the first time in far too long."

Maxa smiles, a blush of evident delight coloring her face. "If you want to feel more alive yet, come back and attend the show this Saturday night. I'll ensure you have an excellent view of the proceedings."

"Wonderful," I answer at once. "I will be here."

"I will see you on Saturday, then. Mademoiselle…?"

A fleeting scent of spice, her perfume perhaps, and my eyelids flutter before I force myself to maintain her gaze. "You may call me Anaïs."

"Until then, Anaïs." Maxa drops her cigarette and crushes it beneath her heel. "Stay safe," she says, and with that, she turns and retreats through a side door. I am left alone on the street, the yellow sun beginning to lower over the distant rooftops.

Even now as I write these words—Hugo lying asleep beside me, with the dogs huddled in the corner upon their pillows, the fire crackling in the hearth—I cannot escape the fathomless pools of her brown eyes. Flecked with swirling amber, they threaten to reduce and absorb me beneath their mystical gaze. Surely I am coping with June's absence by forming a schoolgirl fascination with another woman, what Dr. Allendy might refer to as sublimation. Regardless, the thought of Maxa and her enveloping attraction is too alluring and powerful to repudiate.

My hand travels down my chest, across my belly

and to the inside of my thigh, and I touch myself there. My fingers seek out the wet folds, the sacred core of my being. I count the days until my return to the theatre, the holy temple of nightmares and lust that awaits me as its own breathless lover. I count the hours and minutes as well.

∿

On Saturday night, I return to the Grand Guignol. There is a single ticket waiting for me at the box office, as if Maxa knew I would be alone, sensed my need to open myself to her without the distraction of a companion. Either that, or she wanted me all to herself.

I settle into my third-row seat and leaf through the evening's bill; last week I had left my program behind thinking I would be returning from the intermission, only to be swept away by Hugo and his abrupt and demanding amorousness. This time I find her picture, the size of a half-page with her face in profile as she peers over a pale and exposed shoulder. Examining the image leads me to believe I may indeed have seen her on the stage in the past, though I have no specific memory of it. No wonder, really, as everything inside the theatre seems so very different now, as if I am glimpsing it all through new eyes. The house lights lower, the audience applauds before hushing, and I once again fall under the spell of the Guignol.

After three preliminary productions—a comedy of mistaken identity that takes place at a nunnery, followed by a harshly realist play on police corruption and an elderly couple evicted and thrown into the street, as well as a sex farce in an overgrown greenhouse in Marseilles—it is time for the bill's featured attraction. *La Famille du Péché*, the title printed in the program's largest lettering. The Family of Sin.

The curtain opens onto a dimly lit stage, where a girl of perhaps eighteen is asleep in bed. She rolls back and forth in the sheets, and as she does so a bespectacled and middle-aged man enters. He approaches on the tips of his slippered toes, a flickering candelabra in his outstretched hand, and he slowly circles the bed. He peers down admiringly at the sleeping girl's figure, and reaches across the bed to stroke her long hair upon the pillow. At last she rouses, and she stares at him in wonder and doe-eyed confusion.

"Father?" she says, and sits up with the bedsheets clutched to her chest. "What are you doing in my room at this late hour?"

"I came to check on you, my darling. To make sure you're not suffering too much on this cold winter's night, what with the stove heatless and in need of repair."

"I am quite cold in here, it is true. Would you lay with me, and help make me warm?"

"Oh yes, of course. I will lie with you all night, if that is your wish."

The father rests the candelabra on the nightstand and pulls back the sheets, climbing into bed beside his daughter. He presses himself against her back, runs his hands up and down her arms, along her sides and her narrow frame, until he starts to undo the buttons at the front of her nightgown. Is it a trick of the imagination that, for a fleeting moment, the man resembles my own father Joaquín? That the daughter he touches in such a seductive manner might also pass as a younger version of myself? I shift in my seat, newly unnerved.

"Father," the daughter whispers, aghast. "What are you doing? This is against God's will!"

"Come now, my pet. You know what it is I am doing, why I came to your room this evening. Just as you are aware that you have matured into an exquisite womanhood, and have blossoming desires of your own. You know what it is I want, because you want the very same thing yourself."

"But…but what if Mother should hear us?"

"That old cow? She was in the wine all night, and fell fast asleep long ago. We have nothing to be afraid of, nothing in the world. Believe me, dear daughter, this is just as God intended. Now, lie down on your stomach. Go on."

He finishes undressing her. Soon, he enters her from behind, his trousers dropping to the floor as he thrusts against her. "I have never felt this wonderful before!" the daughter cries, her bared breasts dangling from the foot of the bed as he continues rutting away. "Is this what love is meant to be, at last? If so, this cold winter's night never end!"

A square of dim light materializes on the wall, upstage from the bed and the incestuous pair. An opened doorway, filled at once by a shadowy figure, and the audience murmurs in equal parts trepidation and excitement. From the wings steps Maxa, barefooted and clad in a silk robe. Wild-eyed and crazed, she gazes cursed upon this scene of perverse and unspeakable horror, one beyond any real mother's sane comprehension. She slowly approaches the bed, as father and daughter proceed heedlessly in their dance of lust and forbidden desire, oblivious to her ghastly presence.

"Are you warm yet, my little darling?" the father pants, bent over his daughter and grasping hold of her breasts in his large hands. "Can you feel me hot inside you?"

"Oh, yes," she answers, "yes," and she arches high her body, the carved figurehead of a mermaid rendered upon the prow of a ship. "Keep warming me, Father. Keep warming me! And promise that you'll never stop."

"I promise, sweet daughter," he says, his eyes rolling back in his head as he approaches orgasm. "I promise…"

"You dare!" Maxa thunders. The blaspheming pair separate and scramble away from each other, toward opposite sides of the bed. "Such flagrant sin and depravity, under my roof? The only warmth you'll know is from the infernal pits of hell itself!"

She takes the candelabra from the nightstand and dashes it to the ground. In a loud rush of wind and heat, a blast of heat and light explodes from the front of the stage, and the crowd gasps as a scrim of fire leaps along the footlights in a barbed circle. The vindictive mother throws her head back and laughs a damned laugh, while father and daughter shriek in terror as the bed appears to go up in flames. I lean back in my seat, amazed by the effect, another of the Guignol's astonishing stage illusions.

Maxa lowers her head, her contorted grimace dancing in the bright flames. Her righteous gaze falls upon mine, and our eyes meet through the wall of fire, her stare so piercing I am forced to shut my eyes from the sight of it. When I open them again, however, it is my own mother who stares down at me, just as surely as it was June that I saw upon the operating table last week. Only this time, I do not peer out from the audience, but rather from the stage itself. Now, I am looking out from inside the terrified daughter's burning body, my mother beside the bed and laughing at my well-earned pain.

Panicked, I turn to face the audience. I glimpse myself seated in the pew, where I smile back through the wall of fire. Or is it Maxa who smiles from behind my eyes, using my very own lips? I lean forward, but the heat from the flames causes me to retreat, and I hold my breath in abject terror.

The curtain closes, and with a sudden snap of heat

and light, I am back. Returned to my seat and to my body, in time to see the curtain shut from the audience, my view of the stage occluded as if by storm clouds shuddering across the moon. The crowd cheers all around me, and I clench my hands together, palms wet with perspiration. I cough and struggle for breath, and swallow at the air as if I am drowning.

♋

AFTER THE SHOW is over, I wait nearly an hour for her to appear outside the theatre. Finally, the stage door groans open and Maxa emerges, accompanied by her fellow actors, two men and a woman. I recognize them from the cast, the father and daughter from *La Famille du Péché* as well as a gentleman from the greenhouse scenario, who also had the role of the lascivious goat herder during my last visit to the Guignol. I stand stiffly nearby as they bid one another goodnight, and the younger gentleman, the goat herder, offers to walk Maxa home.

"That will not be necessary." She points her chin in my direction. "I have somebody waiting."

The other actors disperse, and Maxa approaches.

She puts a cigarette to her dark red lips, which I light before lighting my own. "Thank you," she says with an air of nonchalance I first mistake for superiority, but soon recognize as being closer to inevitability.

"How do you do it?" I say, no longer sure who or what it is I am dealing with, be it woman or something else altogether. "How did you capture me in the performance tonight? Draw upon my private thoughts, so that you were able craft that deviant scenario to begin with?"

Maxa exhales in a whistle between her teeth, smoke dispersed in the dim shine from a nearby street lamp. "Everyone sees what they want to see," she answers at last. "Especially the lonely, and the self-consumed."

"You play at knowing me. My hopes, my dreams? My passions. You seem so very sure of yourself."

"If only that was the case." She smiles. "Perhaps everything you saw tonight was a fantasy of your own making. You, who wants so desperately to be a part of something larger than yourself that you forced a connection to the piece, one in which you could live out your darkest desires. The association between you and the performance was only in your imagination. A simple delusion."

"That was no delusion." A drunkard staggers across the street, bleating out a tuneless rendition of "Parlez-Moi D'Amour," and I wait until he is out of earshot before I continue. "I could feel the flames upon my skin, the starchy touch of the bedsheets upon my bare flesh. Not only that..." I swallow hard, draw deeply off my cigarette while I wait for the words to order themselves, for their meaning to become clear. "I could feel a once-empty space shift inside me. It was as if I were making room for you, as if we became undifferentiated, two individual souls fused together as a single spirit. I feel it even now."

"Go home," Maxa says. She stares down the block, in the direction of the drunkard stumbling his way around the corner. "While you still have a chance for it all to make a strange kind of sense, so that you may pack it deep down in a solitary corner of your memory and forget we ever met. Tell yourself that you were simply tired, or anxious, that you were enthralled by the great horrid spectacle of the Guignol to such an extent that it overwhelmed you. Perhaps you drank too much, or you fell faint, like so many others before you. Make a story of it for yourself, one satisfying enough to put it all out of your mind. Just go. Now."

Her words resound in my ears like a pagan incantation. Instead of repelling me, they have the effect of a soothing balm, patching over the prickled shock of experiencing the unexplainable. An offer to forget, to smooth my harsh edges as one would polish an unearthed gemstone. I shake away the sedating effect, however, and focus with a renewed sense of purpose. This offer, it is for her benefit, not mine. If she rids herself of me, then she will no longer have to submit to human connection, to her own raw vulnerability. I know this kind of woman all too well.

"I shall do no such thing." I take another step closer to her, near enough to kiss. "Not until you tell me who you really are, and how you were able to entrance me with whatever strange magic you are capable of conjuring. And I will not leave you be until you do so."

Maxa shakes her head, dark curls grazing the collar of her coat. "Some secrets, once fully excavated, can never be reburied. Once you cross certain thresholds, the journey cannot be unwound." Unmoved, I fold my arms across my chest and we stand in silence. Finally she sighs, a smoky laugh hissed between her lips like steam from a boiling kettle.

She flings her cigarette into the path of a passing motorcar. "Walk with me," she says, and juts out her elbow, offers me the crook of her arm. Another woman once offered me her arm here for the first time: June, who slipped her hand over mine as we made our way to a café in Montmartre. More than a year past, a frosty winter's night that kept the pair of us pressed close to each other. June proved an enchantress herself, though one of an altogether different nature.

I lock my arm in hers, and Maxa and I proceed together down the rough cobbled court, walking as one into the chiaroscuro labyrinth cast over the crisp spring night.

∾

HER APARTMENT IS only a few blocks from the theatre, and we walk at a brisk pace. Maxa often looks over her shoulder, or stops to peer into the faces of passing strangers, as if she is attempting to glean some hidden meaning from their features. We soon reach her building, the last of a succession of severe tenements, and climb the stairs to her top floor flat.

Once inside, I take in the dark living space, an

eerie reflection of the Guignol's sensual morbidity: black velvet draped in heavy folds along the walls and ceiling; all the upholstery blood red, from the tattered divans to the throw pillows atop rugs in teetering piles; elaborate oversized candelabras, whose immense pillar candles Maxa lights one after the next, dried wax suspended in hardened pools across the scored wooden floorboards. She pours us two tumblers of pastis, kicks off her boots, and drops down onto one of the couches.

"Sit, please." She hands me a glass, and I lower myself across from her, nestling upon a pillow beside the tiled hexagonal table at the center of the room. She gulps at her drink, lights a little brass lamp, and fishes a strangely shaped pipe from among the unseemly items splayed across the table. "Would you like to smoke opium with me?"

"I…I never have before."

"Then pay close attention." I watch fascinated as she leans over the lamp and inhales the dark brown tar, sweet blue smoke emerging from her lips and floating upwards, restless spirits made visible. Her eyes close in rapt pleasure, and I feel that I have become vestigial, someone who has seen her safely home to the sheltering arms of her true lover, one capable of meeting all her needs.

I take the pipe from her and inhale, the smoke floral and spiced as it invades my lungs. I hold it in, then exhale it in a wide arc. "And now you have smoked opium," she says. "I did warn you that were crossing a threshold."

She sighs, her heavy eyelids drooping upon their beds of powder and kohl. "You asked me to tell you how I was able to access your mind, to commingle our essences on the boards at the Guignol. You asked how it was possible to see out from the eyes of another. But in doing so, you ask the wrong questions. If you really want to know how I am gifted with such talents, then you must learn how it is that I reached this twilit pass."

Maxa pours herself another pastis, the glass clouded the way her eyes are clouded, murky and unforthcoming. "In more than fifteen years at the Guignol, I have died thousands of deaths upon its stage. I have been stabbed, strangled, poisoned, hanged, scalped, burned alive, buried alive, and more. An impressive achievement as far as such things go, no one can deny that fact, and believe me when I say that each death has been felt deep inside me. Every one of them, from the first to the last."

She sets the opium alight, draws in the thin line

of smoke, and hands me the pipe so that I may do the same. This time I become lightheaded, and try not to cough as I exhale.

"These little deaths, they take their toll," she says. "Upon my body and mind, my very soul. No part of me left untouched or uncorrupted, nothing left of me pure. So it is that in turn, I myself have killed. Murdered, as I have been murdered. For lust, for revenge, in defense of my womanhood: varying forms of rightness or injustice, meted out however the Guignol playwrights see fit. These killings do their own type of damage, and I dwell in a dual darkness of my own making, trapped in a tangled web of violence as both spider and prey. In doing so, I have become the very bride of death itself. There is no escape. Not any longer."

She casts her eyes about the room, as if seeing it for the first time. The mutable shadows and flickering candle flames, the dense fabrics womblike and suffocating, all of it a haze through the dense scrim of smoke. "This apartment was once my safe haven," she whispers. "It was filled with sunlight, with laughter. With the sweet smell of fresh flowers threaded through the air, a home suffused with hope. But then a man came along, and he changed everything. He led me

away from the sun, and soon all my hope was gone."
Maxa shrugs. "These days, I am a reflection of the
world itself, from which hope fast departs just the
same. You feel it as well, do you not? The entire globe
will be drenched in blood soon enough."

"Surely you can find your way out of this," I say,
taken aback by the unending depths of her despair.
"Surely there are other theatres who would consider
themselves lucky to have an actress of your obvious
abilities. Or there are other lines of work to pursue.
You needn't be tied to the Guignol and its perverse
charms. It is not as if you are some kind of indentured
servant."

"But that is exactly what I am." She smiles, though
there is no joy in it. "Only it is not to the Guignol that
I am enslaved."

Maxa lights a cigarette before her eyes settle on
mine once more. "There is a man who walks these
streets, the one who stole me away from the light and
brought me into darkness. A most dangerous man,
cruel and unyielding. He wears black from head to toe,
so that he may go unnoticed, until it is time for him
to reveal his true face. He goes by many names, and
also by no name at all. To some, he is the Dark Angel

of Music, whereas to others he is known as Crocell, Lord of the Great Deep. But I know him as Monsieur Guillard."

She glances behind me, into the heavy velvet folds draping the walls, as if expecting to see someone there. "I called upon him once, when I was younger and reckless, and he came to me, as a midnight lover arrives. With a snap of his fingers, he made all my troubles vanish. My profound pain, my loneliness, my hunger? All of it was lifted from me, in a whirlwind of lightning and rain. I never felt so happy, not in all my life. I became Maxa, High Priestess of Sin and Horror, the Crown Princess of Blood.

"I'd found my purpose at last, and my ascent at the Guignol soon followed. As my talents blossomed, I grew capable of casting glamours and charms, like the fairies of legend. I learned to make my face beautiful one instant, and hideous the next. I could even cast a spell to cause a crowd to feel what I felt in that very moment, to look out from behind my eyes. Draw on the audience's hidden fantasies and perversions, to make each role a revelation both personal and profound."

"That is how I witnessed my friend in you the other night."

She nods. "Another gift, from the Dark Angel."

"That is how tonight, during *La Famille du Péché*, that I saw my own..." I do not say more. Though she must already know what dark thoughts stir inside me, what forbidden passions loom behind my mask of propriety. She must know me, now.

"At first, it felt as if they were gifts given freely," Maxa says. "It was a golden time. One in which I made my own name, and was freed at last from the shackles of my childhood and the rest of my unhappy past. Then one gloomy spring night not so very long ago, a night very much like this, Godfather Death finally showed me his true face. I had almost forgotten about him, which made it all the worse when he darkened my door once more. He came to collect his payment, and I could not refuse. Now, I fear I do not have very much time left at all. That is the nature of such bargains, I'm afraid."

"What is it you owe this man? Perhaps I can secure you the necessary funds to help ease your debt."

"Money." She chuckles, her eyes receding into her skull as she slides further into the opium's poppy embrace. "You do not understand. He has no interest in such concerns." She holds her cigarette to her lips, the smoke bisecting her face. "He only desires flesh,

ROBERT LEVY

in all its many forms. He is the demon lover, and what isn't given to him freely will be taken by force. I attempt to appease him. To sate him, the very best that I can." She glances at the pipe upon the table. "Still, it is never enough."

A firm rap jolts the apartment door. Once, twice, three times, and her face goes ashen pale. "No," she whispers. "Jesus in heaven, no."

"What is it? Is it him?"

"Not tonight, please, not tonight." She rises from the couch and stumbles over the corner of the table as she falls moaning to the carpet. "Please, no, not now. Not now."

"I will protect you." I help her back to her feet, my mind soupy and swimming with the drug. "I will not let him bring you any harm."

"There's no protecting me from him. Not now, and not ever."

Another three knocks, louder this time, more insistent, with the fraught menace heralding the arrival of a villain from the wings. And how we seem to have found ourselves cast in just such a scenario, as if written for the Guignol stage itself! Whether I prove heroine or victim, it is still too soon to tell.

"Quick," Maxa says, and hands me my bag. She shoves me toward the wall, inside a parting in the dense black curtains. "Hide behind here. Once I lead him to the bedroom, you must depart immediately, and hurry straight home. Whatever you do, do not look behind you. Do not see him for what he truly is. Promise me that."

"I promise." I slip between the dark folds. "Do not worry. I will go straight to the police."

"The police can do nothing to help." Her haunted eyes fix me in place. "If he finds out you are here, that will be the last of me on this earth. And it won't end there. It never does." She closes the drapes, and I am left entombed inside the black walls.

The stutter of Maxa's footsteps as she makes her way across the room. The clatter of the latch as it is undone. The creak of the door as it opens. After an excruciating silence, footfall as the threshold is crossed, one deliberate thump, followed by a second. The door groans closed, and I hold my breath, the velvet lapping against me in black liquid waves.

"Maxa?" The unfamiliar voice is a nighttime invocation, a multilayered harmony that is both young and old, masculine and feminine, and my skin prickles with gooseflesh. "Is there someone here with you?"

"No," she answers quickly, too quickly. Heavy footsteps proceed into the room, steady and precise, a soldier amidst his marching drills as the stranger opens and closes a door somewhere across the room. This is followed by a second door, and a cabinet or wardrobe door. As he navigates the room, it becomes apparent he is searching out a potential interloper, searching for *me*, and I am sure my pounding heart will give me away. All this I hear from the cocoon of lush darkness in which I have found myself, so close to detection and stiff with fright, and utterly unable to act.

I smell him on the other side of the curtain. A man's scent, musky and ripe, but also the smell of the sea, salt and semen and sweat, the aroma brutal and intoxicating in equal measure. I list, and I am flooded, returned to Allendy's strange box and the conjured man that walked from the waves, the ocean rushing over me in a relentless tide.

The black material flutters, and though frozen with fear I force myself to one side as the curtains are parted. A sliver of light against the wall, and the cracked plaster is illumined in a gash of bright yellow. His breath is hungry and rasping and wet, that of a ferocious animal on the prowl. Gloved hands hold open the velvet folds, fingers startlingly long and thin and deathly black. I am unable to breathe.

"There's no one here," Maxa says from the other side, her voice tremulous, so much so that I am sure she has given me away. Yet the hands withdraw, the curtains fall back into place, and the firm thudding of his feet reverberates as he retreats, followed by Maxa's own reluctant steps.

A door opens deeper inside the apartment, and I wait for some time before I dare to peer from my hiding place. The living space is abandoned, and I clench my bag to my chest and tiptoe across the room to the front door. I take hold of tarnished brass knob, an array of photographs and clippings pinned to the wood: a prayer card of a female saint on her knees, a pamphlet for a perfumery advertising various discounted scents, a portrait of a voluptuous young woman seductively posed on her back, this last image affixed to a ragged shred of wallpaper, the pattern a field of blood-red anemones.

From down the hall, the primal cadences of great abandon issue forth: grunting and slapping and whinnying, the moist sounds of lips and hips and coaxed flesh. I remove my hand from the knob, and turn to face the corridor and the gaping darkness beyond. Down the passageway, the animalistic noises surge in strength and severity, uneven walls panting and undulating in their own heaving breath, in, out, in. I start down the passage in a somnambulant daze, my mind fogged as I look up to find I have reached the end of the hall, the door here ajar. I peer through the breach, a narrow seam of light slashing across the rumpled bed. I should never have come here in the first place. I know this, and still I cannot obey.

It lies atop her, the thing I mistook for a man. Naked and bestial, its shoulders are impossibly broad, tapering down to a narrow waist and meaty buttocks. The whole of its oil-slick skin is coated in a wet down, almost milky in the diffuse light from the tapestry-covered window. Its crown carries a faint suggestion of a ridged skull, hanks of long black hair strewn from its head across the stained silk pillows in a cascade of seaweed-like strands.

I step further into the room. Beneath the beast, Maxa squeezes her eyes shut, her hands grasped tight to its sweat-slicked hide, clinging fast for dear life. Her mouth is slit open the way the door is slit open, her upper lip bloodied at its corner as if chewed at or otherwise bitten. I creep toward the bed on a wave of devouring intensity and hover above their wild and rutting forms. I reach for them, fingers extended to take hold of the beast's heaving back. To what, intercede? To free Maxa from its brutal embrace? To join them? I cannot say for sure.

Before I make contact, Maxa startles to attention. Her eyes go wide as they settle on me, her expression animating with surprise but also with a savage fury. At once, she propels naked from beneath her possessor and cries out in a banshee wail. "Get out!" she screams at me, manic as she beats at my face with her fists. "Get out, get out, get out!"

I sink against the wall, attempt to shield myself as she batters about my head with a series of kicks and punches, until I manage to stand once more. I thrust her to the floor and scramble over her prone form and back toward the door. As I move past the bed, the beast atop it raises its head, snout to the air as if searching out a scent. Though its features are obscured by its damp sweep of hair, I glimpse two small knots of coiled bone upon its scalp, and my blood turns to ice.

With a languid and elegant gesture, the creature extends a long arm in my direction. It is as if it means to beckon me closer, or perhaps impede my escape. I force my way to the door, staggering out into the dim light of the hallway. In my opium haze, I am left to wonder what it is I have truly seen, whether the drug has made falsehoods of the observable world.

The harsh squeal of bedsprings, and I race to the front door and fumble with the knob, my hands no longer functioning as they should. A blur of movement down the hall casts violent shadows at the edge of my vision, and I finally manage to fling the door wide. I slam it fast behind me, and stumble down the stairs and across the landing as the door creaks open above. I don't look back, and descend the next flight and the next, spiraling down into the dark pool of night. When I reach the bottom, I pause to glance back toward the stairwell, into the constricted throat that winds upwards like the contours of an ammonite shell, like the corkscrewed horns growing from the heavy crown of the beast's skull, savage and impossible.

From the very top of the twisting stairs, someone or something stares down from above. I cannot see well in the dim, only a silver-yellow glint from two gleaming eyes as the figure retreats further into the shadows. I stifle a cry and hurry through the vestibule and out of the building, and rush into the street to hail a taxi. Soon, I am on my way back home. To Louveciennes, and my husband, my garden, my life of safety and comfort, and even my own quiet kind of happiness I seem so determined to destroy. I sink my heavy head in my hands, and breathe in, out, in, willing myself into logic and reasonableness. But logic and reasonableness never helped anyone before. They certainly never helped me.

Though the effect of the opium has already started to fade, my perception of the world around me has altered nevertheless. As I write in this diary and dawn breaks on the other side of the drawn shutters, these once-smooth pages have coarsened and become less pure. Even my handwriting is unrecognizable to me, as if penned by a different hand, this skin worn by a different person altogether. Now, as it begins to rain over Paris and its outskirts, I watch Hugo as he shifts and turns in bed beside me, his sleep troubled. Who is to say what has become of him in my absence? Maybe he has suddenly changed forever, and is no longer the man I once knew. Who, indeed, have I become to him? Or even to myself?

I am haunted by Maxa. Her wild cries as she

battered me, yes, but also her frozen face as she lay beneath the beast, eyes shut tight and unseeing. I am desperate to free her of her burdens. To endure them as my own, no matter her refusals or refutations. If only I was innocent enough to bear them, noble enough to claim I only want to save Maxa from herself, the way I once tried and failed to save June.

In truth, I must admit there is more to my desire to take on the weight of her debt. For my dark and shameful secret is this:

I want to be the one beneath the savage beast.

∽

A few days later, a letter from Maxa arrives at Louveciennes:

Anaïs,

I am writing to thank you for the kind note you sent to the theatre asking after me and inquiring about my wellbeing. I also wish to extend my deepest apologies to you, in the hope that you will forgive me for what transpired the other night. I was not in my right mind, and never should have exposed you to such illicit matters. It was never my intention to corrupt you, and for that I am most sorry. Allow me to explain myself just a little further, after which we must cease all communication, despite (or perhaps because of) your obvious and heartfelt concern.

I am a very closed person, and indeed you are the only soul of late who has so much as glimpsed behind the heavy veil that obscures my defective heart. Since early in life, I have associated pleasure and pain, and it is this truth that has brought me to the place I am today. The games of doctor and patient as a little girl, in which my flesh would be pierced with needles as we played at inoculation? The summer trip into the mountains that culminated in the loss of my innocence, by means of a brutal attack by the young man I had called my closest friend? It was only natural that I would eventually find my way to the sinister side, called to worship by the midnight muse himself. He who walks at night, who traverses the lamplit streets of this city, under cover of darkness and always on the prowl for his next conquest. Is he not the very same phantom rumored to haunt the Palais Garner, the one who inspired Leroux's novel?

The demon lover is no fiction, however. He is as real as we are, a creature of supernatural attraction that beckons to women who are lonely and artistic and most of all passionate, women who radiate the energy he feeds upon until glutted. Woman like ourselves. While I myself am a lost cause, you still have a chance to find your way free, and I pray that you will choose a different path, and allow yourself to feel worthy. You, who have so many admirers, none of whom will ever fill the void within. I recognized the emptiness inside you, the way only someone with the very same absence could see it. Only you can fill that void, Anaïs. It took me much too long to understand this truth. I cannot deny I see myself in you as well. We are parallel souls, rooted in a sensuous attraction to the forbidden. You have kept your urges largely hidden, however, from yourself as much as anyone. Do not forget, I am able to pull back the veil that obscures your private desires, just as readily as I can remove an evening glove. And what I see in you is a past rooted in perversion and degeneracy, regardless of how much of it you mask in the trappings of polite society.

The absent friend you glimpsed in my face that night at the Guignol, the woman who holds your heart in her hand? The father who came to you as a child, the one whose attentions you still crave, no matter how far you go to bury it beneath the hard and cracked ground of denial? You need to be possessed by another, in order to feel anything whatsoever. That, and more.

I had hoped to take comfort in your welcoming arms, but instead I must entreat that you never think of me again. To dwell upon the darkness is to open a door through which it can enter at any time. Eradicate me from your memory, lest you meet a danger you are unprepared to face. And should you ever cross paths with my tormentor, make certain that he never learns your name. Names have great power, in our world as well as his. You must remember this above all else.

Now I must bid you farewell, sweet Anaïs.

Thank you for your kindness, and know that
I will hold you in my heart as Persephone did
Orpheus, no matter my moonless destination.
Light a candle for me, and pray to all that you
hold holy.

  I remain yours,
  Maxa

I read the letter once more before I refold the pages and tuck them inside my diary, smooth the creased paper until it is sharp enough to draw blood. Maxa is done with me. Regardless of the circumstance, I cannot help but sense an echo, a recurrence, as if June is abandoning me all over again. My father as well, as Dr. Allendy would no doubt remind me had I returned to him for further analysis. My life, it is a wide spiral, made up of alluring figures that emerge from the darkness to penetrate my orbit before they are flung out to distant shores, distant dreams. The same story told over and again, until the spiral completes another circuit and a new face emerges from the gloom.

THE BRIGHTNESS OF the noonday sun bears down upon Les Puces, where Hugo and I walk through the marketplace's labyrinthine assortment of stalls, the smell of fresh lavender and saffron threaded through the air. Porte de Clignancourt and the surrounding neighborhood is swollen with shoppers, and I wait in the shade beneath a canvas awning while Hugo tries on carnival masks for a masquerade his supervisor is throwing in a few days' time. Attendance, unfortunately, is compulsory.

Weeks past now since the disturbing events at Maxa's apartment, and though I have heeded her appeal to leave her be I cannot help but feel a coward, unable to put any of it out of my mind as she asked. How can I rid myself of the image of those cruel eyes as they stared down at me through the darkness? The same yellow eyes from Allendy's box, and the taxi outside the Guignol, watching with hunger as a hawk watches for quarry. The eyes of a demon.

Worst of all is when I look into the mirror, where I am terrified I will find those slick yellow orbs staring back at me in place of my own. Perhaps this inscrutable creature has been watching me all along and it is only now that I am aware, its gaze penetrating me to my hidden recesses, the core of me. Or perhaps the truth is something more alarming altogether.

"Anaïs? Darling?" Hugo waves me over to the booth, the beaked white mask of a plague doctor held to his face. "What do you think of this one? Is it too garish?"

"If anything, too respectable." I scan the rest of the mask-maker's offerings and select a more colorful option, that of a damask joker done in flamboyant points of gilded crimson and gold. I help Hugo fasten it behind his head. "Now, you look fit for a proper night on the town. Still elegant, yes, but not so dour."

"You mean, I no longer appear quite such a bore." He returns the plague doctor mask to its peg. "Would that I had the ease you seem to have, the ability to travel between worlds. You have a keen talent for moving freely through various social milieus, and seemingly without care."

"Is that how you see me, as a chameleon? Someone who changes their face in order to adapt?" I cannot help but feel as if he is mincing words. That he means to call me Janus-faced, willing to alter myself to meet the expectations of others.

"Do not take umbrage, my love. I was trying to

pay you a compliment." He smiles and takes me by the hand, and we continue to wend our way through the market. "I was speaking of your generosity of spirit, and the interest you show in those you encounter. I see it in the way you make conversation, as readily with street performers as you do with the wives of my colleagues."

"The wives of bankers bore me, though. Never mind the fact that I am one myself."

"But you never let your boredom show. Through it all, the essential Anaïs is ever-present, thrilling and excitable and attentive. That is why others are drawn to you, no matter their circumstance. You are independent, and alive. Another reason why I am so proud to call myself your husband, why I love you and you alone."

He pulls me into his arms, and we kiss. "And I love only you, Hugo."

And now I have told the lie. However much I admire my husband, there is always someone else. Always.

Hugo wears a wide smile upon his face, and I attempt to mimic his aura of insouciance as we near the far side of the market. A strange niggling sensation pricks at me, however, and I feel as if I have forgotten something, or someone. I glance behind me, back toward the mask-maker's booth and the canopied stalls beyond. Someone is out there, watching.

From some distance away, a dark-haired woman gazes at me through the bustling throng, and I slow my pace. Dressed in black and awash in radium sunlight on the periphery of the market, pale and thin and birdlike in her delicate pose, my first thought is that she appears lost, and perhaps afraid, a solitary figure beside a meat vendor's display. It is only when I cease walking altogether that I realize I am looking upon myself. Into a standing mirror, of which there are many set out for trying on items of clothing or jewelry. But no. The woman that is me reaches a slow hand to her brow, long pale fingers raking through her corona of black hair. Yet here I am, holding Hugo's arm with one hand and my market bag in the other. There is no mirror there after all.

"Anaïs?" Hugo peers over at me in concern. "Is something wrong?"

"That woman," I sputter. I take my hand from his arm and point in her direction. "Do you see her? There. Just past the meat counter."

"What woman?"

"Her! Right there!" I gesture all the more frantically. "The one there, in the black dress."

"I don't see her," he says, and shields his eyes from the sun as he scans the crowd. "Who are you talking about?"

"For God's sake, Hugo." I drop the market bag, a cascade of oranges toppling out and across the dirt. "She looks just like me."

The woman turns, and I follow. I push my way through the throng and past the mask maker's booth, where in my haste I knock a red leather harlequin mask from its peg. Hugo calls out to me but I don't stop, hurtling forward as I struggle to keep my eyes upon her, the woman in black that is myself.

Only yards away now and just outside the main thoroughfare of Les Puces, and she returns my gaze once more. Now I see her for what she is: her flesh a pallid and mottled blue, lips black and bruised, skin brined with deep ocean water, the dregs of the abyss. She is a drowned woman, this other Anaïs. She is still myself, yes, only after the sea has swallowed me.

My likeness—*ma semblable, ma soeur!*—moves quickly along the meat counter. She rounds the far side, and I hurry around the stall, only to find that she has vanished. The space where she should be standing is now dense with the sticky sweet smell of kief, as well as an incongruous scent of the seaside.

"Maxa?" I whisper. Is this some conjuration of hers, an attempt of hers to communicate with me? What then of her entreaty that we cease all contact? The vision has evaporated, and left me standing in the drowned woman's place.

"Darling?" Hugo, out of breath, places a gentle hand on my shoulder as I scan my surroundings in vain. "What is it? Is everything all right?"

"It is nothing." I shake my head furiously, as if trying to shake away the incident itself, wipe it clean from my mind's uneven slate. I tell myself it was an aftereffect of the opium, but I know it was something else, something inexplicable. It has left me with a lingering and disturbing anxiety. Perhaps I have had a premonition of my own death.

I calm myself as the butcher's wares swing above me, gruesome hunks of pork ribs and pettitoes lashed to wires like sacrificial offerings to a bloodthirsty god. Everywhere I look is carnage. All I am able to do is hold myself, and I stare up at the overcast sky. "I thought I saw someone I knew."

"You gave me quite a fright." He hoists the market bag beneath his arm. "Shall we be on our way, then? Emilia is preparing pheasant, and I offered to deliver the oranges to her."

"That sounds lovely." The words are distant and foreign, spoken in a stranger's voice, as if through another's lips. "Let's go."

I take Hugo's arm, and we reenter the market through the crowded stalls. When I look back, there is no one watching, and we continue on our way.

∾

WE ARRIVE AT the masquerade in darkness. Fairy lights are strung across the property, lending the evening an otherworldly feel, as, of course, do all the many disguises worn by the guests. Hugo is costumed as the sea king Neptune, bare-chested and adorned with glittering scales affixed to his sides that run up his neck and across his eyes in their own kind of mask. I am Venus arisen from the ocean deep, my breasts covered by two large clamshells, smaller shells woven into the hair pieces that obscure my bare shoulders in golden waves. We are, as they say, of a pair.

Trident in hand, Hugo ushers me through the lush garden, the air warm from a flickering bonfire and reverberating with animated conversation. Blood-rhythmed music echoes across paving stones and through the gnarled crepe myrtles as a band performs atop a raised platform, masked couples swaying on the temporary dance floor laid out across the packed grass. Our hosts, dressed as a monk and a nun, come down from the patio to greet us. A passing waiter offers champagne from a lacquered tray, and though I take a flute I am already made drunk due to the raucous surroundings, the dizzying whirl of light and sound and carefree revelry. As Hugo and our hosts make small talk, I scan the garden, take in the many costumes: the satyrs and nymphs, ballerinas and chained prisoners, an impressive Louis XIV and Marie Antoinette in their own gilded masks. The mood is giddy, the guests shielded and hence emboldened by their chosen disguises.

Across the dance floor, a solitary figure watches me. A man, tall and broad-shouldered and dressed in old-fashioned naval fare, his tricorne hat pointed cowl-like like a bird of prey's savage bill. Dark paint upon his face glistens beneath the lights in an iridescent wave, narrow eyes barely perceptible but for a silvery yellow flicker upon them, cast from the fairy lights overhead. A frisson of excitement spreads across my arms and bared stomach, my thighs beneath my diaphanous skirt, commingled with an unnerving charge of fear. He nods, and tips his hat in my direction.

I take a tentative step back, and look away, over to where Hugo and our hosts should be. Except they seem to have vanished farther into the garden, somewhere past the wide nettle of trees that ring the impressive grounds. I return my attention to the naval captain, who departs across the dance floor through the swirling sea of dancers, silent and unseen as a wraith as he makes his way toward the main house.

I follow in pursuit. Slowly at first, but then I hurry to keep up, my sandals slapping loud against the stone steps as I reach the patio. A cluster of guests chat near the open doorway to the house, a waiter returning from the kitchen with a tray of food, and as I enter the foyer I glimpse a pair of black-booted feet ascending the staircase. I trail after him, and take the steps two at a time, only to find the hallway empty. I pass from room to room, the whole of the house filled with the aroma of boiling coffee and steamed milk. Another scent as well, the burnt spice fragrance of Maxa's flat.

ROBERT LEVY

Another set of stairs, and by the time I reach the top I am in near darkness. The party below is a quieted lull, and I think of the seaside and the susurrus of waves, rolling in, out, in.

I feel my way along the hall for a light switch, and though the way forward is cast in shadow it is free from impediment. At the end of the corridor is a dim and narrow room, lit only by moonlight from a small round window, the roof bowed like the ribbed hull of a ship. I am reminded of being a little girl, and of leaving France to sail across the ocean to America. Indeed, the scent of the sea is unmistakable, the air thick with a wild and salty tang.

Across the room, a figure emerges from the shadow, and what little light from the window is obscured. My breath catches, and I try to reach for the doorknob, only to find myself unable to move. The stranger approaches, his tricorne hat indistinguishable from his face, his head, his body, so that he is at once a man and a being of irregular angles, his true dimensions difficult to discern. He towers over me, a wall of darkness born out of a larger darkness more impenetrable, vast and unknowable. In a flash, he is at my side, the rough fabric of his suit jacket abrading my bare arm as he reaches to close the door with a soft click.

"What is your name?" It is him, the man from Maxa's flat, the beast disguised in human flesh. His voice fathomless and yet mellifluous, an alluring combination of softness and steeliness, of pleasure and pain commingled. I shudder, and for a moment I cannot answer.

"My name?" I say, and swallow hard. "My name is... Maxa."

"You are not Maxa, no." A heavy sigh, rattling and luxuriant, and above all laced with hunger. "I know Maxa. You are someone else altogether. Your own creature."

"What...what do you want with her?" I begin to say, but "Shhhh," he whispers. I am silenced. A gloved hand caresses my cheek, and I pull away. I imagine myself leaving, backing through the door and down the stairs, out of the house and across the garden and through the city streets until I am safe at home in Louveciennes. I do no such thing, however, for I am already entranced. The time for leave-taking has passed.

"Tonight is a masquerade," he says. "And so you can be whomever it is you choose." He uses a single finger to guide my face toward his. The leather is supple against my skin, and the tip of the finger parts my lips and slides across my teeth before he removes it. "Tell me, then. Is it Maxa that you truly wish to be?"

"I would never wish to be her," I manage to say, my mouth dry. "Not when she is enslaved, captive to forces beyond her control. Not when you are her soul's tormentor." I want to run but cannot, legs trembling and unsteady like those of a newly birthed fawn.

"Tormentor? Hardly." He chuckles, low and hoarse. "You insult me, and yet it is you who invited me this evening." He touches one of the shells affixed my chest, his finger tracing its scalloped edge. "Even now, you adorn yourself with the very tokens of my realm."

"That is not true," I whisper. But of course it was my suggestion that Hugo and I wear these costumes inspired by the sea, incited by my waking dream in Allendy's box, the sifted-through contents of my own conflicted mind. I had sought to negotiate with my enduring pain, and in doing so I unknowingly invited danger to my door.

"I only grant that which is desired," the stranger says, his tone the low thrum of a wind instrument, the prayer of a parched desert landscape for the salvation of rain. "Do you know what it is that you desire?"

His finger presses against my cracked lips. I swallow hard, and snake the tip of my parched tongue over the leather, which tastes of rare and exotic spice.

"I do know," I say, my open hand against his midsection, hard muscle beneath starched wool. "I do."

"Yes." He places his hand over mine, fingers interlacing with my own. "I know what you want as well."

In an instant I turn and am against the closed door, my body firm against the wood. The whole of him leans against me and I gasp, the door rattling in its frame as his other hand slides between my legs and yanks my underwear down with a quick thrust. My skirt rises, and I steady myself against the door, bracing for his penetration. He lowers himself behind me, however, his tongue at the opening of me, and I widen my legs as far as my tangled garments will allow.

He sucks my clitoris into his mouth, and I bite down on my hand, still pressed against the door. The smell of brine, and the boat that is this room lists so that I am face down on the deck as a wicked squall swirls all around. The sky black, the sea black, everything swallowed whole in a heavy blanket of endless darkness. My thighs slick with a honeyed wetness so powerful I convulse.

He is devouring me.

I want to be devoured.

"Anaïs?" Hugo's voice, muffled and calling from somewhere beyond the door. "Anaïs, are you up there?"

I try to arch my back but I am fixed in place, speared against the door as my body is wracked with a ferocious sensuousness. I bite down on my hand harder, lest I go mad.

"Anaïs," the stranger whispers from my hindquarters, his graveled voice its own aphrodisiac. "What a beautiful name."

"Please," I whisper, the sound of footfall on the creaking stairs through the wood as my husband approaches. "Please, I have to go."

I wrest my hand from his, reach down and yank up my underwear. As I do so my fingers graze his hat, and the tricorne falls free. In the faint moonlight, his hunched form is massive, bestial. His head remains lowered, face shrouded in a nest of wet black hair, from atop which emerge the two gnarled horns I glimpsed in Maxa's bedroom. Now the stranger slowly raises his head, and emits a deep and snarling laugh, his wicked pair of coltish yellow eyes flashing through the dark. What I see of his face is a savage amalgam of leonine features, the proportions of which lend the impression of a second face straining against the first.

The room judders and cants, and I fumble for the doorknob. I finally manage to free myself, and stumble into the corridor before shutting the door fast behind me, my skin burning with stirred desire.

At once I slam into Hugo, who drops his trident as he places a hand on my waist to keep me from falling. "My darling, what is it?" he says, his expression unreadable. "What's wrong?"

"I feel feverish," I manage to get out. "Something must be coming over me. Would you mind if we went home?"

He raises an eyebrow, his glitter-bedizened face contorting with suspicion. "Were you in there with someone?"

"Of course not. Shall we go downstairs? I would like to leave now."

"Is there someone in there? Let me through." Hugo retrieves his trident and forces his way past me. He throws wide the door, and when he turns on a lamp the room is illumined in an electric white.

It is only a simple sewing room. Hugo marches inside, and I hold my breath as he searches the small space from end to end, nothing about it resembling a boat whatsoever. There is no one here, neither person nor creature, and I cannot account for what occurred in this unassuming place, its own kind of sealed room. I do not know whether to feel relieved or tormented, whether my encounter was the result of a demonic visitation or simply a fantastical creation of my own fractured mind.

"See?" I cross my arms over my chest. "Now do you believe me?"

"Of course, my darling. I apologize for overreacting." His expression slackens, and relief colors his cheeks. "Are you sure you wouldn't like to rest for a few minutes? Can I get you something to drink, perhaps? I am sorry you are not feeling well."

"Do not trouble yourself," I say, and shut the door behind us. "Everything will be fine. I am feeling better already."

I feign a smile, and curse myself for deceiving him. I may be a practiced liar, but soon I will become a prodigious one, and eventually Hugo will be unable to see through my deceptions to my authentic self.

"Shall we?" I take his arm and lead him down the hall, my thighs damp with saliva and my own fevered excretions. We descend the stairs and rejoin the party, our fellow revelers blind in their merriment to all that walks among them.

❧

I WAKE IN the night and reach for Hugo, only to find the space beside me empty. And so I step out of bed and throw on a negligee, the dogs fast asleep before the cindering hearth as I slip out of the room and down the stairs in darkness. In the strange, crepuscular shine through the windows, I make my way to the front door, which I discover has been left open. I cross the threshold, the air heady with the scent of night flowers as I enter the garden, the grass beneath my bare feet slicked with cool dew.

I realize now that I am dreaming, and stare back at the house and its wide face, its eleven shutters closed to the evening like slumbering eyelids. All save the center shutter, which is thrown wide, the glass of its window visible in the moon's mellow glow. The sealed room has been opened.

The soft crunch of wet leaves, and I turn. There is a slight figure adjacent to the elm tree, past the drive and the far side of the fountain. A crouched and half-hidden shape, barely perceptible in the blue moonlight but there nevertheless, not ten yards away. I am too scared to move any closer, and yet I know I must puzzle out what is happening, that the answer will comprise the most important truth I have ever known.

"Maxa?" I whisper. Perhaps she has decided to pay me a visit after all, here in this twilit realm. "Maxa? Is that you?" The figure shifts behind the tree so that it is hidden, and I force myself forward. One foot before the next, and it takes all my courage to make the slow and inexorable walk to the tree and the fleeting shape beyond.

When I finally reach the elm, I travel counterclockwise around its formidable trunk, its branches swollen and dripping with moisture. There is no one here any longer, and only now do I realize I am holding my breath. I exhale a cloud of perfumed smoke and lean against the rough bark, my relief laced with a disturbing sense of unease, the source of which I cannot place. I close my eyes, and listen to the trill of a nightingale chirruping in the heavy leafage above.

"Have you forgotten me so soon?"

The stranger's molasses voice shocks me to attention. A melodic baritone spoken everywhere at once, as if sung by a midnight choir of the damned. I attempt to run, but my spine is adhered to the bark, fixed to the elm's rough trunk like a fly drowning in amber. My hands stick to the tree as well, and I thrash and struggle as I try to free myself. Soon, however, I am immobilized altogether.

"Come." The invisible fiend whispers into the shell of my ear, the disembodied word seductive, ravenous. "There is so much more I want to show you."

The heavy branches quiver and bend, and the elm's dense and unseasonal greenery ripples and descends, draping me in a foliate shroud. I am forced against the meat of the tree, pressed into its bark as if into wax. The pressure increases, and I flail in terror, my gaze rearing up toward the house and the darkening sky beyond. At the open shutter, I see the slight figure once more. This time, she stands in the window of the sealed room, her small face staring down at me as I struggle against the tree.

It is myself. Or rather my younger self, maybe nine years old, my tiny hands pressed to the glass and following the proceedings below with an inscrutable interest. Behind my younger self is my father Joaquin, who looks down upon me as well, his gaze conveying a similar stony fascination. He stands very close to her, too close, his large hands on her shoulders, body pressed against her back the way the tree is fixed to mine. He is invading her just the same.

Invading me.

Rather than being crushed against the tree's unwavering mass, I begin to pass into it. My flesh melts against and inside its expanding trunk, until the tree has swallowed me.

Once absorbed, I am released, and drop down onto a ground of coarse sand. My racing heart begins to slow, and I get to my feet, alone inside a humid and dimly lit cavern. The wet surfaces are made of pocked shale or perhaps some kind of coral, the distant echo of crashing waves reverberating against the walls. I shuffle my way toward a slit of light cast upon the far side of the cave, and suck in my breath as I wriggle through the narrow egress.

At once, a vast sheet of churning gray light blinds me. After a few moments my eyes adjust, and I discover I am perched atop a carved pillar of uneven stone. The crude slab rises from the bed of a flooded grotto, the puckered bowl of craggy earth draped in gauzy mist and carved from an eroded cliff face over what must be untold millennia. There are more pillars on the shore around me in a rough approximation of a circle, reminiscent of the pylons of an abandoned dock. A large wave crashes over the enclosure, the impact spraying upward in an angry fan before spilling out and away, back to the rocky shore and sea beyond. Above the smell of the salted sea is another scent, that of incense, and I become lightheaded with the holy aroma of sacred space. Another crash, and I throw my arm over my face to shield myself from the angry water. The tide recedes once more, and when I steady myself again, I find I am no longer alone.

Roosted upon the other pillars are a collection of unmoving figures. Two or three dozen of them, women, mostly, though there is a man or two scattered among them. Of varying ages and shapes, every one of them bound with their hands clasped behind their backs, all naked and frozen in the formal poses of classical statuary. They are all blindfolded, eyes obscured with the same tattered material used to bind their hands, the dirty cloth tied in crude knots. One of them is standing, while another is seated, a third crouched, yet another curled onto her side in a fetal position. All are motionless. The roar of the sea, the screeching of famished gulls wheeling overhead, and the battered headland is alive with a charged menace.

The anticipation is broken by a low blast. The blare of a ram's horn, or the keen of an unknown animal, the sound skirls over the encircling cliffs. A shadow appears at the slim parting in the cave walls, long gloved fingers extending and emerging to take hold of the rock before the towering shape emerges. He is attired in the dark loden skins of a sea creature, a dreadful hooded face beneath coiled horns, an uneasy commingling of human and animal. It is the man from the masquerade, Maxa's tormentor, and now my own. He strides toward me in his patchwork armor of ambergris and black leather, and whether to call him man or beast is of little consequence. I decide he is either a thing that was once a man, or perhaps a creature in the process of radical evolution, soon to become something unintended by Mother Nature herself.

I think to leap from the pillar, only to find that my own hands are bound behind my back. I am also naked as well, and aside from the absence of a blindfold I could be any one of them, another bound effigy set out upon a rock as if in sacrifice to Poseidon himself. His narrow yellow eyes focus upon me, and I look away, down at the spot between my feet where I would stare when I was a child and my mother would berate me, furious at whatever fresh shame I had brought to her doorstep.

The creature nears, calcified feet clopping like hooves over the wet stone, the snap and crunch of shells and stones and mermaid's purses as he rears up and leaps with ease to an adjacent perch. He lands with a hard thud of bone upon rock, and takes hold of one of the frozen women by the waist. Only this woman stiffens, resisting his grasp as he pulls her closer. Her feeble effort to squirm free causes him to smile, a flicker of the cruelest face of humanity in his delight.

His hands, which I had thought sheathed in a shiny black material, are in fact formed this way, fingers hooked like deadly talons. He slides one of them down her stomach, through her dark thatch of pubic hair and down between her bare thighs. My eyes return to her face, and I know this woman: it is Maxa herself. She is fixed in a paralyzing rictus, her anguished expression familiar from both the Guignol and her flat alike.

"Release her at once," I command, my voice weak and unassuming. His smile widens at my lackluster demand.

"Why would I do such a thing? She is luxuriant

with feeling, is she not? As am I," he says, the taut animal skin at his crotch straining as he grows engorged. "She chose to join me. To become a part of greater things, surrender to a sensuous realm that overflows with a dark voluptuousness. The same way you have given yourself over to me."

"I chose no such thing," I say, with as much volume as I can muster. "And if Maxa made any sort of pact with you, I can assure you that she was unaware of the terms."

I chafe against that which binds me, but my ties fail to loosen. "What are you?" I ask. "Are you man or demon? Or are you both? What am I to make of you?"

He smiles once more, and my blood runs cold, naked skin turning to ice in the suddenly frigid wind. "I am many things," he says. "Many things, to many people. You may call me Monsieur Guillard."

He leaps across our divide and lands beside me with a hard thud that shakes the stone beneath my feet, the smell of his animal musk commingling with that the sea, the same intoxicating admixture that captivated me earlier at the masquerade. It is a continuation of the very same exchange of pleasure and pain, a *danse macabre* performed as a *pas de deux*. He can find me anywhere, at any time that he desires, and this dance will continue as long as he wills the music to play.

"What is it that you want?" I whisper. "Tell me, and it shall be yours. Only let Maxa free. I beg of you that."

"You know what it is I want." His hand caresses my breast, skin prickling as he presses himself against me. Slick wet fingers travel down my body to my pelvis, until he finds the moistness between my legs. "I want the light inside of you, sweet Anaïs. As I once craved the light inside them," and he sweeps a gloved hand toward the cliffs and the statues dotting the shoreline, all the many bodies forever suspended in their disturbing tableaux.

"You sought this very same annihilation," he continues, his words a menacing rumble. The sky darkens with clouds, voice accentuated by a heavy rumble of thunder as a storm rapidly approaches from the sea. "Like them, you came to me seeking oblivion. And now that you have tasted it, there is no turning back. For oblivion has already tasted you."

He hunches down, his mouth traveling my skin, and my gaze drops to the ground. There upon the sand lies a scattering of shards, and it is only once my eyes focus that I recognize them as the fragments of a sculpture, the shattered remnants of one of the women. The pieces are large enough that I am able to piece them together in my mind, and glimpse the woman that they once embodied, her face long and equine like that of a Modigliani.

I stumble and rear back, and in doing so I face the cave mouth, where the woman with the Modigliani face watches from the darkness. She raises a finger to her lips, her wrist cuffed by torn cloth, though her binds are severed. Another figure hovers in the shadows behind her, an older woman, stooped and emaciated. What I can grasp of the older woman is weathered and formidable, hair a tangle of matted knots, her sticklike limbs corded with muscle and adorned with an array of beaded bracelets of turquoise and amber and gold. She holds a finger to her lips as well, imploring me to remain silent, lest their presence be given away.

I shift my body toward Maxa. Her blindfold is gone now, and she raises her head high, cheeks glimmering in the overcast light. Her once-obscured eyes are sewn shut, wisps of silver thread at her temples. Her jaw drops open and continues to lower, unhinging to an inhuman length so that her mouth becomes its own vast cave. As I watch in horror, she emits a savage cry of terror.

I awaken in my bed, a scream upon my lips. Shuddering and cold, I place my hand upon Hugo's back, his bare shoulders still shimmering with glitter from the masquerade. I want to wake him so that he can hold me and comfort me, tell me that my terrifying encounter was only a dream. Only a dream, a dream. But not a dream alone. A dream also tells the truth, the same way fiction tells the truth, once it is distilled from reality. The same way I use this diary and my emotions and experiences as the fertile foundation for my stories. Indeed, there no longer seems to be a difference between dream and reality, between fiction and real life, as the barriers between realms are shattered one after the next.

Soon, the sun will rise over Louveciennes. Over the city of Paris proper, the whole of the continent and the waking world as well. Come morning, I must have a new resolve, make myself into a new form of creature myself. This being must be capable of resisting the embrace of my would-be tormentor Guillard, of vanquishing this brute birthed out of the vast and wine-dark sea, lest I succumb to the unknowable depths of his nightmare realm. And if I write this new resolve into being, it becomes a kind of truth itself. In order to transform my very life, the diary must turn grimoire. I must become my own sorceress at last.

I cling tighter to Hugo, who can do nothing to help me at all. Only I can save myself, now.

∾

THE NEXT DAY, I return to the Guignol. The main entrance is unlocked, and I let myself in, the heat of the day diminished as I leave the bright sun for the dusty gloom of the former chapel. At once a woman's blood-curdling cries echo across the empty foyer. My stomach knots and I tighten my cape as I hurry forward, sure that I have found Maxa in her final moments, that the midnight fiend that stalks us both has set himself upon her once more.

When I enter the theatre proper, however, I find two players, a man and a woman, mapping out a scene upon the stage amid their rehearsal. Of course, the scream was part of the act: any number of ghastly cries are bound to echo against the walls and ceiling and balcony of the Guignol, on any given day and hour. I linger at the back to watch, beside one of the private boxes that functioned as a confessional when this building was still a chapel.

"Louder, Hélène, louder!" the director barks from the front row, cigarette smoke spewing as he gestures with abandon, his hands glimmering with rings on every finger. "The audience is only going to find the lighthouse keeper menacing if you increase your hysteria. Remember, his face has already been slashed by now."

"Louder. Of course. I understand."

"Then do it again, please," he says, his tone softening. "I've already had enough headaches today."

After a few minutes, a stage manager emerges from the wings. He uses the small set of stairs to step down into the pews, and he approaches me. "This is a closed rehearsal, mademoiselle," he whispers curtly. "I am going to have to ask you to leave."

"My apologies, but I am a friend of Maxa's. Is she here?"

"Unfortunately, no. She has missed the last three performances. We had to call in her understudy," he says, and casts a baleful look at the actress onstage. "If you see her, please make it clear that Monsieur Jouvin is in a rage, and that he plans to let her go if she does not return at once. He is well aware of her vices, and any irresponsibility will no longer be excused."

"I will let her know," I say, the wind going out of me. "Thank you."

Once I leave the Guignol, I hurry to Maxa's place. I hope against hope that I will find her there, that she has not been harmed, or indulged in too much opium for her body to withstand. I ring the bell, and wait at the door to the building. When a distractible family exits the premises, I scuttle inside the vestibule and climb the stairs to her flat.

"Maxa?" I call as I knock on her door. "Maxa, are you inside?" I turn the knob, surprised to find it unlocked, and I slip inside. "Maxa?" I call again. "Maxa? Are you here?"

The apartment emits a chill of loneliness and abandonment, as if no one has been here in quite some time. It is dark as night here as well, the windows and walls draped in their heavy black velvets. I creep down the hall to the bedroom, terrified of what I might discover. That I might find Maxa bound and bloodied, tied to the bedposts in a grotesque display of gore and punctured flesh, a scene of blood-drenched Guignol staged by the unforgiving hand of Monsieur Guillard.

The room is empty, however, rumpled bedsheets

the only vague reminder of the carnal scene I had witnessed when last I was here. I search the flat as best I can, comb through her drawers and her cosmetics kits, determined to find any clue as to her whereabouts. Did Maxa manage to flee, as is my profound wish? It is true there is no overt sign of struggle, yet I am no detective, and I wonder anew about contacting the police.

Though what would I say if I did? No doubt they would point to her opium consumption as confirmed by the Guignol, confirmable by anyone who may have crossed her path. Maxa was correct: the authorities would be of no use whatsoever.

Just as I am about to take my leave, one of the pictures pinned to the back of the door flutters to the ground, and I bend to retrieve it. It is the photograph of the young woman in a lace slip, curvy and Amazonian and luxuriating upon a red divan. Something about the woman's ambivalent expression—how it is both welcoming and observant, the eyes vulnerable and unpitying in equal measure—causes me stare at her image for some time. Who is she?

And all of a sudden I know. The young woman standing in the mouth of the cave, her binds untied as she watched from the shadows, an imposing older woman

ROBERT LEVY

lurking just behind her. The one whose statue was shattered upon the rocky sand, whose face resembled a Modigliani, and I bring the picture closer to my face. The woman on the dark beach, and this woman in the photograph: they appear to be one and the same.

My fingers tremble, and I drop the picture into my bag, nerves frayed like the thief that I am. One final glance about the flat, and I take my leave, the heavy door groaning as I shut it fast behind me.

∿

HENRY AND I lie in bed, our limbs tangled in the sheets. We hold each other, and watch lazily as dust shivers and dances in the afternoon light that filters through his filthy apartment window. He hums a little song beneath his breath, and I try to keep my mind from Maxa's disappearance, as if this routine of false normalcy will keep Monsieur Guillard from my door. The Dark Angel himself. His disturbing face haunts me, as does the possibility that I conjured him without understanding or intent, perhaps in the very same manner as Maxa. But how exactly?

There is a change in the atmosphere, and it takes

me some time to realize that Henry has ceased his humming and fallen silent. I look over at him, and he squints back at me with a bemused concern.

"Little bird, little bird, where did you fly?" he says, and he gives my arm a little squeeze. "You haven't been your playful self lately. Not in bed, and not on the page either."

"I am sorry, Henry. It is just that I have a great deal on my mind."

"Don't think I haven't noticed. It's like fucking a rubber doll, you know? No offense."

"Can a rubber doll do this?" I pepper his face with kisses, his lips, his cheeks and nose, the bald crest of his skull, testing if I can break him of his worry. But when I withdraw, Henry's expression remains unchanged.

"You going to tell me what's going on with you or what?" He leans up on his elbow, as if preparing himself for a lengthy response. I sigh, and sit up myself. Henry knows so much of me, there is no denying this. More than Allendy or my cousin Eduardo, perhaps even more than Hugo. What I have experienced of late, however, is another matter entirely. How can I begin to explain to him the transgression made flesh that walks among us? That a night creature in the guise of a man has come for me in both this world and his own, and now threatens to consume me altogether? These are matters that even a man of Henry's great experience would not be able to comprehend.

"It is one thing to be under the sway of another," I say, an attempt to speak in our common tongue of metaphor and myth, the language of symbol and allusion. "A man, say. Or even a woman," for he knows that I remain entranced by June's lingering spell, just as surely as he does himself. "It is quite another to be haunted by a being that inhabits another world. An angel, or a demon, a creation of light and darkness that cannot be escaped or denied. I have fallen under the influence of such a creature, one I cannot properly begin to fathom. In turn, my life has become a waking dream from which I cannot fully rouse."

"So you're hung up on someone. What else is new?"

"You do not understand my meaning."

"Well *pardonnez-vous*, Madame! Maybe you're just shutting me out with all this mumbo jumbo because you don't *want* me to understand. Ever think about that?"

I get up from the bed. "Maybe it is because I know you are incapable of it."

He reaches for me but I shrug him off, and go into

the bathroom to wash myself. I shut the door and run a wet cloth over my face, my breasts, between my legs. All the places where Henry has been, with his hands, his mouth, his penis. My pleasure with him here in Clichy, this once precious place, noticeably dimmed. The same way Louveciennes has grown colorless, Hugo along with it. I know it is because of Monsieur Guillard. The monster that fills me with an evil and unspeakable poison, my usual pleasures steadily drained from the world around me until there is nothing left but the empty husk of a life once lived to its fullest.

I emerge from the bathroom to find Henry seated on the edge of the bed. He stares down at something in his hands, my bag lying open on the pillow beside him.

"So, is this the lucky lady?" He holds up the photograph from the back of Maxa's door, the portrait of the voluptuous young woman upon the divan.

"Who gave you permission to go through my possessions?" I snatch the picture away from him. "If my husband can manage to respect my privacy, I expect nothing less from you."

"Hey, hey, take it easy," he says, and holds up his hands in surrender. "I'm just looking out for you, alright? Let's just say you better make sure June doesn't find out about this girl. Take it from me. She skips town with a broken heart, and you turn around and fall for a whore? Wouldn't exactly make her feel like the belle of the ball, if you catch my drift."

"A whore?" I yank my bag from the bed and tuck the photograph back inside. "What on earth are you talking about?"

"That woman in the picture. She's a professional." He clears his throat. "I don't want to go into any great detail here. Suffice it to say, that's one of Louisa's girls, over at 32 Rue Blondel. Ask me no questions and I'll tell you no lies. It's not a good idea, that's all."

"You do not understand."

"Yeah, you've been saying that a lot lately."

"Listen to me! I do not know this woman, but she might be in grave danger. Regardless, she may well have information about a missing friend of mine. I am going to need your help, Henry."

"Anything you want, kid. You know that."

"All right, then." I straighten up as tall as I can make myself, allow Henry's gaze to travel the contours of my body until his eyes return to my face. I place my hands on my bare hips, and I smile. "I want you to take me to the Rue Blondel."

THE TAXI LETS us out at the mouth of the narrow little street. I take Henry's arm as we make our way to the unassuming building, the number "32" painted in red over the door. He knocks three times, pauses, then knocks three times again, after which he shares a smile both sheepish and mischievous, that of a naughty little boy. The door cracks open, and we slip into the darkness within.

The *patronne* swiftly shuts the door behind us, and we follow her down a crooked hallway to a wall of heavy and torn red curtains, which she parts as she ushers us through with a sly smile of her own. The high commotion of the room envelops me. The acrid smell of smoke and stale spirits, a tinny waltz playing on the phonograph, and above all the laughter of women, who sit naked at various café tables and along the oak bar. A dozen of them or more, dark and pale and every shade in between, drinking and smoking and carousing in stockings and heels, their buttocks and breasts and mounds of wiry pubic hair on proud display. I blush at the banquet on offer, and turn to Henry, who watches me closely beneath the low brim of his hat.

"Like anything you see?" he says. "We're here already. Don't see why we shouldn't kill two birds with one stone, if you know what I mean."

"We are only here to talk," I say, as I scan the room. "You can return to play some other time."

"Suit yourself," he says, and shrugs. "You're the one who's paying."

Two prostitutes approach, and cling to the both of us in a clumsy attempt at seduction. We send them away, however, and circle the room in search of the woman from the photograph. When we fail to find her, I summon over the *patronne* and show her the picture.

"Ah, yes," she says, and nods. "She is one of mine. Her name is Sonia. Unfortunately, she is not working this evening."

"Do you know where we might find her? It is quite urgent." I return the photograph to my bag and produce a handful of bills. "We will compensate you most fairly for delivering us to her."

"But of course." The *patronne* bows in deference, and guides us to the uneven staircase. We follow her up, the sounds and sights and smells of the café setting dissolving below as we reach the landing and continue to the next flight. Here in these dim warrens, any private desire imaginable can be negotiated and consummated. Or so I had once thought, before I encountered Monsieur Guillard.

Harsh grunts and other rutting noises resound beyond the thin walls, the contradictory scents of perfume and sex hanging heavy in the air as we reach a door at the end of the hall. The *patronne* knocks rapidly before she produces an iron key from her apron. "Please," she says, and holds her palm open. I hand over the money, and she bows with an obsequious flourish before unlocking the door, only to turn on her heel and head back down the stairs.

The room is softly lighted, a red glow from a silk scarf hung over a lamp atop a decrepit armoire that gapes open from the corner. Beside it is a rumpled bed and a cluttered night table that bears an almost-drained bottle of *Le Peau Verte*. Two half-emptied glasses and a bowl of sugar cubes as well, alongside a variety of accoutrements.

Barely a moment passes before the woman in question staggers naked from an adjoining room. She is busy pinning her damp hair, arms held high so that her large breasts heave as she works. It takes her some time to register our presence, and which point she freezes in her pose, her own kind of statue.

ROBERT LEVY

"What are you doing in here?" Sonia reaches for the dresser and takes up what appears to be a simple hair comb. With a flick of the wrist, however, the comb snaps open to reveal a deadly steel blade disguised in its ivory encasing, which she now brandishes with what can only be described as a world-weary familiarity.

"Whoa, lady!" Henry, ever the gentlemen, leaps in front of me. "Take it easy there. Who comes to a cathouse looking for a fight?"

"Did Louisa let you in? I told that bitch I'm not working tonight," Sonia says matter-of-factly. "You will have to find another girl to entertain you."

"We are not here to be entertained," I say. "My name is Anaïs, and this is Henry. We are looking for answers about a friend of mine. Her name is Paula Maxa. I found your photograph in her apartment, which led us here to you."

"Maxa?" She raises a thinly painted eyebrow and snaps the blade closed before flinging the camouflaged weapon back onto the dresser. "What do you need me for? You can find her over at the Grand Guignol in Pigalle. She is probably on stage getting tortured by a psychopathic dentist as we speak. If you hurry, you can still catch the show."

"Unfortunately, Maxa has gone missing."

"Missing? What do you mean, missing?" she says, her voice uneven. "Maybe she took a lover. Everyone needs a break from the world now and then."

"No one seems to have seen her for few days now." I hand her Maxa's letter. "I think she might be in terrible trouble."

"She's flown the coop," Henry says, as Sonia scans the letter. "Sounds to me like she's dug herself a hole she can't get out of. Either that, or someone's dug a hole for her."

"No," Sonia says, and thrusts the letter back at me. "I cannot hear about this now. Not now!" She sinks against the wall until she is curled in a ball on the floor, her hands raking violently through her straw-colored hair until I am afraid she will tear it from its roots. "I already paid my debt," she mutters beneath her breath. "I won't be made to do it again…"

"Henry." I go to him, my voice dropping into a whisper. "Do you think you can give us some privacy?"

"Are you nuts? I'm not leaving you alone with her. Her pupils are the size of dimes. She looks like she's whacked out of her mind!"

"She may be under the spell of the green fairy,"

I say, and cast my eyes toward the night table. "That only means she requires a gentle hand. Regardless, your presence is only going to upset her."

"There's not a lot this chick hasn't seen by now. Trust me."

"Be that as it may, this occasion calls for a woman's touch."

"Fine, fine. I'll be downstairs, checking out the merchandise. But don't take too long, okay?"

I close the door behind Henry and settle on the floor beside her. "Sonia," I begin softly. "Do you know what might have happened to Maxa?"

"It is nothing I can properly explain to you." She lifts her head, her pink-rimmed eyes still fixed on the floor, on whatever horrors her mind has conjured before her. "It is nothing you can hope to understand."

"He is called by many names," I say. "The Dark Angel of Music. Crocell, the Lord of the Great Deep. Those, and more."

Her gaze meets mine, her wide eyes glassy and no less haunted. "So Maxa told you about him."

"Some, yes. But not all."

"She should have kept quiet. Nothing good can come of speaking of him. Quite the contrary." Sonia lights a cigarette, her fingers quivering. "You should pray that you never come face to face with him."

"I have already faced him. He came to me, at a masquerade in Passy. And then he came to be again inside a terrible dream, a dream that was as real as life."

"You." Her hands move to her mouth, red lacquered fingernails tap-tapping against her lips in a blur of motion. "You are the one from the pool of stone. The woman on the shore."

"And you are the one who watched from the cave. The one whose statue lay shattered upon the sand."

She looks to the corner of the room, as if someone else is there. "You are the next of us, then," she whispers. "He already knows your name."

"Yes," I say. "Yes."

"Now I know why Therese wanted to..." Sonia trails off, and quickly stands. She stumbles to the night table, where she empties the rest of the absinthe into a glass. "In a few hours, just before dawn, wait for me at the eastern side of the Barrière d'Enfer," she says, her voice newly firm. "I will meet you there. Make sure you are alone. And tell no one. Otherwise, Therese will know, and then she will not meet you."

"And who is Therese?"

"If you do as I say, then you will find out soon enough." She swallows down the drink with a wince, wipes her lips with the back of her hand, and turns to face the window, the leaded glass grimed with soot. "Now go. And take care not to be seen on the street." I want to speak with her more, but I stand in silence instead, my bag with her picture inside clutched to my chest.

As I cross the room to leave, I glimpse Sonia in the scuffed mirror nailed to the back of the door. She remains frozen in place, her voluptuous form framed in the dirty square of the solitary window as I depart.

∾

I ALREADY TOLD Hugo that I would be remaining overnight in the city to work on the latest pages of my novel. Indeed, I booked a room at the Hotel Anjou and made it available for Henry's use. No one knows where I am really going, however, as Sonia insisted in her instructions. Not even Henry.

Now, dawn fast approaches as I stand alone at the Barrière d'Enfer, and I try not to pace as I wait. The Hell Gate, fittingly, though I have never thought of the pair of austere tollhouses quite so literally. For what other kind of dark journey must I take tonight, save one that will bring me ever deeper into the unmapped terrain of the Underworld? A dark thought enters my mind, that this clandestine meeting is in truth an elaborate plot to draw me into a trap. That this woman Sonia is not aligned with me, but rather has offered me up as a sacrifice. If so, my recent actions have done nothing but hasten my demise, an ending that fast approaches.

The harsh groan of metal, and a small door near the eastern pavilion shudders open a crack, a flicker of torchlight visible through the breach as Sonia emerges from the gloom. She appears focused, no longer the absinthe-addled wretch that Henry and I found earlier at the Rue Blondel but rather the survivor who watched from the cave mouth, her former self left shattered upon the rocky shore. Her eyes are dark pools, narrow and appraising beneath the cowl of a hooded cape. She smiles grimly, and gestures with the torch for me to enter.

I follow her down into an indentation in the earth, the passage paved and stepped like a cellar. I am reminded of my house in Louveciennes and how it has no cellar, how that fact enticed me from the moment I first crossed over the threshold. Something about the way I could feel the earth directly beneath my feet made me feel as if I were a tree capable of taking root, and, despite my distaste for being tied to any one place, I had found my true home at last. As we descend into these sepulchral tunnels, however, there is no such feeling of the earth anywhere near at hand. Here, I am rootless once more.

Past a set of heavy wooden doors, and we travel through a passageway lined with ghastly walls of bone. We have entered the catacombs, the underground network of ossuaries that spiders its way along the tunnels of this vast metropolis. The remains of centuries' worth of Parisians, unearthed when the cemeteries were emptied and relocated to this series of subterranean vaults. Skulls stacked against the walls by the thousands, ornate patterned archways of rib and femur and breastbone and pelvis, a gothic mosaic of generations past. All the many souls of our beloved city, those who lived here and died here, who ate and drank and made love, the reviled and adored alike. In death, we are all the same.

Sonia and I walk for what seems an eternity. And surely dawn has broken by now, the bells of Notre Dame ringing their morning Angelus. Down another series of passageways, the echo of falling water ahead as my guide steps through a circular entrance. It is like the doorway of *Le Monocle*, the women's bar where June once brought me, where she passionately kissed me one autumn evening before we walked home together beneath the stars.

The damp smell of must, and I step over the low partition into a rounded chamber as Sonia halts ahead of me, the torch flame dancing wildly in her hand. Dozens of candles flicker along the walls and floor, threads of wax dripping from atop the crowns of grinning skulls, from within their hollow eye sockets as well. It is the nightmarish scene of a black mass, a dark vision out of Dante or Goya. I tighten my cape around my shoulders, and move farther into the chamber.

At the center of the dim space are two heavy pillars. Between them is a large cistern, from Roman times perhaps, the basin of which catches a steady beading of water that leaks from the bone-vaulted ceiling. In the shadows of the crypt's periphery, a formation of what appear to be statues watches from beneath their own obscuring cowls, arranged about the chamber in a broad circle. Unlike the stone women from my dream, these figures are unbound and clad in moldering black robes. I look closer, and I see one of the hands is that of a skeleton, the white bones of its knuckles glinting in the uneven light. A renewed chill overtakes me, and I hold myself to keep from shivering.

Sonia brings her torch closer to the wall, where a spindly arm emerges from the darkness to grasp it, a stunted form coalescing as if poured from the shadows themselves. It is the rawboned old woman from the dream, the one who watched from the cave alongside Sonia. She takes the torch and places it into the outstretched hand of a cloaked skeleton, before she steps into the quivering pool of light.

"Welcome, Anaïs." The woman lifts her hood, heavy bracelets shifting as her hair springs forth in a wild snarl of unkempt silver. Her face is sallow, skin a papery yellow vellum around a pair of eyes that bulge green and glittering through a sea of dark paint. "My name is Therese. Rest assured that, despite the surroundings, we are safe down here. Thanks be to priestesses past, who charmed the catacombs for this very purpose, so that no demon could walk their hidden paths. At least not the one who now calls himself Monsieur Guillard. Despite his great hunger, this is one moonless place he is unable to haunt, and for that we are most fortunate."

"What of Maxa?" I ask. "Do you know what has happened to her?"

"She is down here," Therese says. "With me."

"Thank goodness." I exhale a heavy sigh of relief. "She is safe, then?"

"Not exactly." The woman nods at Sonia, who approaches one of the cloaked skeletons staged along the perimeter. Sonia lifts the hood that obscures the figure's bowed head, and I gasp.

It is Maxa. Her eyes shut tight, the whole of her frozen as if in the throes of some terrible pain, and I can only stare unspeaking in confusion. She is pale, hair parted doll-like and combed away from her face. To all appearances, she is only asleep and lacks any hint of deathlike pallor, though her chest fails to stir with breath. She is rendered a waxwork, as if she has become her own example of the Guignol's ingenious stagecraft. Either that or she truly is dead, and preserved by a most gifted mortician.

"How?" I whisper. I take hold of her hand, which in her strange stillness I am surprised to find warm, the skin of her palm supple and smooth. "Is she alive?"

"In name only." Therese shuffles onto the other side of Maxa's rigid form. "She has surrendered to

Guillard. Crossed the Rubicon into the realm of the phantom lover, from which there is no return. With much effort, we are able to sustain her body in its present state, but it will not last much longer. If we awaken her, she will begin to decay at once, and soon she will be no more. It would take as little as a day for her to expire. Maybe less."

"What can we do to help her?" I am trembling now, mortally afraid. "What can we do to prevent this fiend from claiming her once and for all?"

"What can we do?" Sonia says beside me. "Nothing." We stare as one at Maxa's corpselike figure. "Maxa pleaded with him to spare her. He only laughed, and called her a fool for attempting to revoke her vows. We saw all this from the dream place, his nightmare realm of stone and sea."

"What vows?" I ask. "Maxa is neither bride nor nun. She made no covenant with him."

"Oh, but she did," Therese says. "We all did. That is why we are here now. Every one of us promised ourselves to him, each in our own way."

She reaches over and caresses Maxa's waxen cheek. "When she was a child, Maxa went for a walk in the mountains with a young man. He set upon her and brutally raped her, stabbed her repeatedly and left her for dead. As she lay bleeding upon the cliffs, she pleaded to God that she be spared. When she received no response, she began praying to a different being instead. Maxa promised herself to him and, in exchange, he restored her to life without injury. As with the rest of us, there was a price, that many years later he came to collect. You must have made a similar bargain yourself."

"Never." I furiously shake my head in refutation. "I never gave myself to him. I would never make a slave of myself, not to any man. Let alone a creature so cruel."

"Not knowingly, perhaps." Therese's voice is gentle, almost pitying. "But the phantom lover is clever. It is when you are at your lowest point that he appears, pen in hand, with the kindly manner of a saint. Always in the darkest hour, when you are most in need of the light."

I think of Allendy's office, of sitting inside the isolation accumulator. How fragile and childlike I had felt, trapped within the box's enveloping darkness. So small again, and so fearful, and most of all so deeply alone. I recall that long-ago time when I was a little girl as well. How lost I was, and how I prayed for my father to return to me. I held so many confused and conflicted feelings inside, over his unwholesome attentions and his eventual abandonment, all of which led me to start this diary.

The diary. I swore myself capable of becoming my own sorceress, that the words I wrote between these tarnished covers could prove powerful enough to bend my reality and reclaim my life as my own. Only what if I have always been this powerful? The words from the diary, they have already proved to carry a fierce power of their own, my desires realized into the real world, that of flesh, and of blood. Did I not wish as a young woman in my diary for an all-consuming lover, a suitor conjured from the shadows of time to fill the void left in my father's wake?

"No. This is not our fault. None of it," I insist. To Sonia and Therese, to Maxa's unmoving form, to all the many dead and watchful faces encircling us. "This is not our doing! Who would punish a young child, or even a grown woman, for seeking answers or love or companionship in her time of need? Our souls might have cried out for help, yes. But opening the door to despair does not give evil our permission to walk through. Maxa did not ask to be consumed by such forces. None of us did. This cycle of madness must end, and in order for that to happen, we must fight back. And we must win."

"He is formed from the roiling deep," Therese says. "That which is made of the whirl of crashing waves cannot be captured, and will always find its way back into being. He is a storm demon, fashioned from the very depths of the abyss itself. He cannot be drowned, or even burned. He can only be endured."

"Then we will come up with another solution." I puff out my chest, make myself as large as I can. "There is a way to end everything, even a creature such as Guillard. Anything made can be unmade. That is what Mother Nature teaches us to be true."

Therese chuckles at my boldness, her beaded bracelets clacking against one another. "You do not understand," she says. "He controls the twilight realm, the place where we saw each other upon the windswept shore. He can come for you at any time there, and do whatever is in his power to do. In his world, you are his to command. That is his home."

"Then we will confront him here, in Paris. The city that is *our* home. And we shall do it tonight."

I play with the strings of my cape, the satin

banding my fingers. "How is it that you are safe from him?" I say. "You, Sonia, whose image lay shattered upon the shore of his domain. And you, Therese, who never appeared captive in the first place. How did you manage to secure your own safety?"

They exchange a look of longing and anguish before Sonia bursts into tears. She hurls herself into her companion's arms, Therese combing Sonia's hair and rubbing her back for comfort.

"Sacrifices were made," Therese says quietly, her eyes unwilling to meet mine. "We purchased our freedom at the expense of others."

"Three girls," Sonia says through her sobs. "Sisters, who worked with me at the Rue Blondel. We summoned the demon, and we gave them to him. He hasn't appeared to us since."

"I am sorry, but I cannot do that." I shake my head. "Neither for Maxa nor myself. I will not offer up another in my stead."

I wait for them to speak, but when they fail to do so I continue. "The Dark Angel, he came to me recently, at a masquerade. He must have felt welcome there, able to operate under cover of the night, his true face hidden from sight. We shall lure him back by promising him more shadows, a place of darkness where he feels most comfortable."

"Do you think you are the first woman to try to destroy him?" Sonia laughs bitterly, and throws her hands up in frustration. "He is not a man, but a demon."

"Then we shall make him otherwise. The way Hera changed Tiresias from man to woman, we shall transform Guillard from demon to man. We will seduce him, the way we have been seduced. Only we shall use the cunning words and the alluring gestures of the coquette, or the virgin, or the courtesan. Appeal to his vanity, the way you would draw forth any man, as the spider lures a fly into its web. And then, like the spider, we shall strike."

"And where exactly do you propose we attempt such folly?" Sonia's eyes widen, with what I can only assume is incredulity. "Where shall we lure the beast to lull him into such submission that he would give himself over to the very women he is so fond of afflicting?"

The crypt falls quiet, the hollow skulls vigilant and waiting. All the many faces of the departed Parisians, who watch as an audience watches, breathlessly awaiting the next twist of fate as our dark drama of violation and revenge plays out before them. It is in them that I find my answer, and smile at last.

∞

BEFORE THE CAR comes to a full stop, Maxa opens her door and steps onto the street, her feet unsteady on the rough cobblestones. I pay the fare and hurry out of the taxi to lend her my arm, and she leans hard against me as we totter our way to the stage door of the Theatre du Grand-Guignol. Already she is fading.

She raps on the wood three times. After a brief pause she raps once again, and I am reminded of Henry's surreptitious knock at the door of 32 Rue Blondel. All the many secret codes and signals, the mysterious pass keys that gain us entry to private places hidden behind heavy doors. Was it only last night that we had ventured out to the whorehouse in search of Sonia? My life entire is now lived in the realm of the incredible, indeed the impossible.

A stagehand opens the door, and upon seeing my wan companion he rolls his eyes with great force. "Maxa!" he cries. "Where the hell have you been? Jack is out for blood." He exhales smoke, his cigarette juddering at the corner of his mouth. "He said if you show your face around here again, to make certain you know that you've been permanently replaced by Hélène."

Maxa straightens up. "You find Jack," she hisses, and I see what a struggle it is for her to marshal her strength, to project her expected air of superiority. "And you make certain that *he* knows it will take a far greater director to get rid of Maxa! Not to mention a better actress than Hélène to replace her." She reaches with a shaky hand to snatch the cigarette from between the stagehand's lips, and she points it back at him, the tip dangerously close to his face. "Now, my dear. Are you going to get out of my way, or am I going to have to put this out in your eye?"

He flattens against the wall, hands held up in submission, and she strides past him. I follow as she staggers ahead through the theatre's narrow backstage passageways, until we reach a cluttered dressing room. "Wait here," Maxa says, "I'll be back," and I take myself inside.

Racks of costumes fill the space. Nun's habits and clerical vestments, corsets and pre-styled wigs, tattered burial clothing and hospital gowns and schoolgirl uniforms and far, far more. Past the racks there is a small and crowded table, the surface overrun with assorted powders and paints and brushes, bottles of cream and pots of paste. The round mirror against the naked brick wall is cracked down the middle, two small lamps trained upon its tarnished surface and casting an unearthly glow. I bend to examine my reflection, turn my face this way and that, searching out any indication of my own potential decay. How calm I appear, given the dangers at hand! By midnight, both of us may no longer be of this world.

As I study myself, the sensation of being watched creeps over me, and my eyes flit across the glass. Cleaved in two by the violent lightning crack upon the mirror, I glimpse an image of the unimaginable standing behind me, that of the most alluring woman on earth. Still as a statue in portrait-worthy silhouette, as if captured in bold aquatint by the deft hand of Matisse, hair pinned to one side beneath a plumed hat, her lingering form rests against the doorframe as she watches me through blazing bright eyes.

I turn and face her. Breath trapped inside my chest, my heart aflutter as I take in her wry smile, her lips painted the color of a ripe plum. With one look, she instantly possesses me once more, and it is as if she had never departed Paris in the first place. Her gaze, as ever, is ravenous.

"June?" I manage, once I have found my voice. "Is it really you?"

"Hello, Anaïs." She steps into the dressing room and glances about with a languid curiosity. She parts her cape to reveal a black silk dress, a new one, the neckline low and matched by a lengthy slit that exposes her gartered and stockinged leg. The extended gazelle limb of a taxi dancer, the graceful dancer she will always be, so long as she still draws air.

June slides aside one of the costume racks and nears with the same air of voluptuous nonchalance she exhibited the very first time I laid eyes upon her, in the garden at Louveciennes. Not much more than a year ago now, but nevertheless an altogether different time, one in which I naïvely thought I understood the boundaries of the world outside my door.

"It's good to see you again," she says, her eyes returning to my face.

"I…I don't understand," I sputter, and it is as if I am encountering a ghost. She kisses one cheek and the other, and I cannot help but blush, the heat of desire pumping fresh blood to the surface of my skin. I had forgotten how much taller she is than me, how delicate and small she makes me feel, a hollow-boned little bird that may be snapped in two with ease. "When did you return to Paris?"

"Early this morning. You don't have to worry, I won't be here long. I'm off to Rome tomorrow. I've been hired to dance in an Italian revue. A legitimate one, I might add."

"I am happy you are here. Only…. What are you doing at the Guignol?"

"A little birdie told me you might be here," she says, and I wonder if she has plucked the image from my mind in her own deft form of sorcery. She unties her cape and squares her shoulders, the cramped room made more so by her heavy aura of imperiousness. "So. Where is she?"

"Where is who?"

"This other woman Henry told me about." She cocks her head. "The actress I hear you've fallen for. She must be something else if she caught your eye."

"I have not 'fallen' for anyone," I answer meekly. "Henry was wrong to tell you that."

"Yeah, well, Henry's wrong about a lot of things, isn't he?" She pulls the chair out from the table and sits. "My feet are in so much pain," she huffs, and begins to loosen her boot laces. "I walked across half the city today. American Express, Café Viking, the usual haunts. All in search of you. That might not mean anything to you anymore, but I wanted to make sure I saw you in the flesh."

"June, please. You must listen to me." I place a firm hand upon her shoulder and hold her in place, the way you would to ensure the attention of a child. "You cannot be here tonight. This theatre, it is not safe."

"Don't you know? It isn't safe anywhere." She laughs wryly. "The world is a great big terror from one end to the next. Always has been, and always will be. Especially for women like me." She extends her long stockinged legs, her feet coming to a rest on the table edge. "For women such as yourself, however? The ones with means, who can afford to keep their heads above water? Well, I wouldn't know anything about that now, would I?"

June gestures toward me dismissively. "Sure, you play at a kind of bohemianism, typing up your little stories while you trade bon mots with my husband. But it's just a fantasy of poverty, of *feeling*. You daydream your life away, until it's safe to go home again to your banker husband, your beautiful house in the suburbs. Because you're free. Free to live in your safe little world, to hide yourself away at the first sign of trouble. You're too fucking sheltered to know real danger."

"Once, perhaps. But no longer." I lean over her, and we stare at each other in the mirror, our faces inches apart. "Since I have last seen you, I have experienced things I have never known before. Terrible things. Believe me when I say that I have felt fear I never thought possible."

"That's what this whole place is about, isn't it?" she says, and waves her hand in a wide circle. "The famous Grand Guignol! Step right up, and have a look at the freaks behind the curtain. The poor, the deranged, the perverse. Get yourself a little thrill, a safe thrill, because nothing here is going to hurt you, not really. That's not real life, though, is it? Because real life is never safe. Real life is *merde*."

She places her hand against my face, long fingers stroking my cheek. "Remember when we came here together?" June says. "You were so excited! Like you were a child again. I could care less, of course. All the fake blood, the phoniness and melodrama. I still managed to have the time of my life, though. You know why? It was because I was with you."

"I think of that night more than you can know." I crouch beside her, and take her hand in mine. "It was as if a hidden part of myself had only just made itself known." I think of the sealed room at Louveciennes, and all the many secrets inside. "It was like nothing I had ever experienced before. Or since."

"I told you I'd do anything you asked of me, if only for a night. And I still would." She smiles again, tears forming in her eyes. "That's because you saw me, Anaïs. Really saw me."

"And you saw me," I say. "We will always have that. No matter what."

A single tear falls from her eye, and streaks her cheek with black mascara. "I wanted us to be together. But then you and Henry..."

"I am so sorry that it happened this way." I kiss the back of her hand, nuzzle against it, hold it to fast my chest. "I never meant to hurt you, you must know that. How I wish things had been different."

We kiss, her wet lips glazed with the taste of raw honey. "I still see you," I whisper, the words their own invocation. "And I always will."

Maxa lurches into the dressing room. Beads

of water cascade from her hands as she closes the door and leans against it with her eyes shut. "All the arrangements have been made," she says in a panting breath, and I wonder if Therese's revitalizing tonic has worn off altogether, if she has even an hour left in her.

Maxa widens her palm beneath the nearest lamp, her fingers blackened with a gangrenous rot. "This entire plan of yours is utter insanity. Even if Guillard does arrive, you'll only have a short time to pull it off before... I mean, would you look at this? I am beginning to fall apart."

She holds her hand this way and that, until she finally notices June, who stares back at her with undisguised irritation. Maxa hides her hand behind her back and waits, wordless. June does nothing to relieve the silence, only looks Maxa up and down as one appraises an eggplant or a cut of meat.

"Who the hell is this?" Maxa finally says, her entire body stiff as a rod.

"A friend," I reply. "June Miller, this is Paula Maxa."

"June Mansfield." She stands as she corrects me, and retrieves her hat from the table. "The pleasure is mine. Unfortunately, I was just about to leave."

"Wait," I say, and grasp hold of her arm. "Maxa, a

moment, please. I need to speak with June."

"Be my guest." She drops into the chair between us and rests her head against the table, her skin sallow in the mirror. "But I don't have all night. As you well know."

"She's really not what I expected," June says to me, staring down with distaste at Maxa's crumpled form. "Nice to see you still like them rough around the edges. Always on the lookout for a fixer-upper, am I right?"

"June, listen to me." I take her hands in my own, and draw her attention back toward me. "What you said that night, about doing anything I asked of you. Do you truly still mean that?"

"Why, are you calling me a liar now?" she says, and scowls. "I thought you knew me better than that."

"Answer me. Please."

"Cross my heart, Anaïs. Whatever you want. You know that's the truth. Honest to God."

"Good. Because I need you watch over me this evening. To act as my guardian angel, no matter what dangers may present themselves." I take June's face in my hands, our gazes locked together. "The Guignol is about to see its most unforgettable evening yet."

ROBERT LEVY

THE AUDIENCE BEGINS to file inside for the performance. I take my place, not in the usual rows but in one of the confessionals at the rear of the chapel, the enclosed and private spaces lovers are known to occupy for their trysts; Maxa has commandeered a box for me. I settle on the bench and close the confessional door, the mesh partition raised so that the theatre beyond is transformed into a chiaroscuro of light and shadow. I look around the dark box, and my pulse quickens. Perhaps it is the ecumenical setting in which I find myself, but it is all I can do not to clasp my hands together and pray for a steadying hand.

The house lights dim, and soon the sharp pull of the accordion ushers us into the world of the Guignol. The master of ceremonies takes to the stage, and it is only once he has done so that I see just how far I am from the footlights, from where Maxa will deliver her performance in only a few brief minutes. There will be no helping her, just as she will be unable to assist me in my own grim undertaking. The roles have been cast, the twin stages set. There is no turning back.

The curtain opens and I force my breath to

lengthen and slow, eyelids fluttering as if I am falling into a waking dream. The first act begins in a classroom setting, Maxa's understudy Hélène as a schoolmistress correcting papers at her desk. A handsome young student peers through the door, his head a halo of auburn curls. "You wanted to see me, Madame?" he asks, and "Yes, George," she replies. "Come in and shut the door, please." He approaches, awkward and stiff, nervous hands clutching a stack of books over his groin.

"What is it you have beneath your books?" she asks, and the audience titters.

"Nothing, Madame," he says. "I swear."

"Do not lie to me." She glares at him over the top of her spectacles. "You are my very best student, but you have been distracted of late."

"I have been distracted, it is true," he says, and scratches at the back of his head. "But that is only because of you."

The crowd continues to laugh as the farce unfolds, and soon the teacher and her student begin making passionate love. Through the crosshatch of the screen, I catch glimpses of their bared flesh: his freckled shoulders as he arches his back to better position himself beneath her, the pale meat of her thighs as she straddles him atop the desk. All the while, my heart races ever faster, the confessional walls are so near I begin to have trouble breathing.

I close my eyes, and caress my face with the back of my hand. Allow my fingers to travel down to my neck and across my collarbone, spidering beneath my cape and bodice, along the curve of my breast. My desire stirs, and I focus on my own powerful sensuousness. It powers an erotic phosphorescence made brighter by the light of others, yes, but always mine to command. It is as essential a part of my being as breath itself.

Come to me, as you came to me before, I sing in silence. My hand slides down my belly to the cleft between my legs. The bench is hard against my buttocks, only a thin sheen of silk separating my flesh from the rough grain of the wood. *Come to me in this still-holy place, and let us share this dance of death together.*

The door to the confessional slides open. A tall figure crosses the threshold and closes the door, the darkness returned. The bench groans beneath his weight as he sits, a cold and heavy hand dropping down upon my thigh. I stifle a gasp as his fingers interlace with my own, and I dare not glance over. My eyes are fixed upon the stage and the carnal scene unfolding, even as my suitor's seawater scent engulfs me, his breath rolling like the tide, in, out, in.

"Hello, Anaïs." His voice velvet, as soft as his shirt sleeve is coarse, the fabric harsh against my bare arm. "I am pleased that you called for me."

"Hello, Monsieur Guillard. I am pleased that you answered."

"Oh, George!" the schoolmarm cries from atop the young man. "You truly are my very best student!" The audience applauds, and she tosses high the work from her desk, a swirl of papers cascading across the stage in a wide arc as the curtain draws closed.

"Ah, how wonderful to be back, in the theatre that Maxa once haunted," Guillard says. I attempt to shift down the bench, but his grip tightens so that I am fixed in place. "She was a gifted performer, was she not? A pity I could no longer sustain her talents."

"How can you say that you sustained her, when all you have done is draw away her vitality? Does a parasite cease leeching from its host, only to claim it an act of charity?"

"Maxa summoned me, and I complied. The same way I complied when you called."

"Tonight, I did summon you, it is true." Though

paralyzed with fear, I want to face him in all my righteous fury. "On that we can agree."

"Ladies and gentleman, may I have your attention," the master of ceremonies declares from the footlights. "We have an unannounced performance this evening. Our very own Paula Maxa, The Maddest Woman in the World, is about to grace the stage in a once-in-a-lifetime appearance that will amaze and astonish you."

"Ah. Maxa." Guillard's face nears the partition, and I look over at him now, silver-yellow eyes narrowing beneath his heavy ridged brow as he gazes into the dim of the theatre. "One final performance, then."

"Oh yes, Monsieur. One final performance indeed. And it is dedicated to you."

"To me?" He grins, a mouthful of silver teeth flaring in the scattered light. "This should prove amusing. I thought Maxa no longer fit to walk this world."

"Her pain, it is intoxicating to you, is it not?" I whisper. "You take pleasure in it. The way an alley cat takes pleasure in toying with its prey, before finally killing and consuming it."

"I do take pleasure in her pain, yes." His fingers feel their way up my body, and he finds my collarbone, where he taps with a single sharp fingernail. "But only to a point. Far be it from me to deny Maxa an end to her suffering."

In a flash, his arm clamps tight about my waist. He pulls me onto his lap, the crown of my skull near the top of the confessional, a narrow band of space between the partition and the ceiling so that the screen no longer obstructs my view of the stage.

"Now, I will possess you fully," Guillard says through clenched teeth, a promise he intends to keep. "I will carve my way inside you, into depths of yourself that you have yet to fathom." His long hand moves up my stockinged leg, my body arching as his fingers slide inside me. "I will possess you to your very core."

"Prepare yourselves for a performance unlike any you have ever seen, not even upon this legendary stage of appalling vice and ruin!" the announcer cries, his hands thrown wide. "Here she is, in a tour-de-force that will defy all reason and explanation. I give you The Most Murdered Woman of All Time, The Crown Princess of Blood and Horror herself, the Great Maxa of the Grand Guignol!"

He steps into the wings as the curtain opens on Maxa at center stage. Lit by a single chalk-white spotlight, she stands motionless in a black dressing gown, her head lowered and face obscured, arms cradling her midsection as if in attempting to hold something inside. The audience stills, the absence of sound deafening as they await that which is to come.

"Possess me then, demon lover." I reach behind me, hands raking fistfuls of his untamed hair until I take hold of the twinned knobs of his horns. "Wash over me, the way the ocean subsumes the shore."

"So it shall be," he says, his words a ravenous taunt as he hardens beneath me. "As the earth relinquishes itself to the tide, so too shall you know what it is to give yourself over. Every part of yourself, each inch, within and without."

"Look!" a patron shouts. A gasp from the front of the house, followed by a series of screams as Maxa lifts her head to face the crowd. Now in profile, a green shadow falls over the curvature of her cheekbone. As I writhe against my would-be conquest, my dress yanked to my waist while he frees himself from his trousers, I am able to view Maxa and her greatest performance of all.

Her face is blighted by a swath of decomposition, a dark green infection that rapidly and impossibly spreads across her skin. Only this decay is no stagecraft illusion, no artful deception to horrify and delight the audience. This time, the disintegration is all too real, as Maxa rots onstage before the awestruck crowd.

Another shout from the pews as Guillard thrusts upwards, and I feel him inside as a frozen and inhuman thing, an icy convulsion wracking me. I grasp hold of the mesh screen, fingers scrambling against the metal interstices. Alternating waves of pleasure and pain crash over me, and my hands curl into fists, the partition rattling beneath my grip. A response to my excited state, yes, but also a cue, a signal to the one who watches and waits from her seat beside the aisle.

A wave of startled screams from the audience, and I emit a scream of my own. My dilated body rocks atop Guillard as a boat rocks upon a storm-churned sea, and I cannot help but moan in response. I am back, back inside the hull of the ship that bore me away as a child. Inside Allendy's box as well, where my most monstrous and hidden desires were transmogrified. I inhale, and the aroma of wet sand and tidal pools and my own ripe sex envelops me in a divine alchemy of scent, powerful and fecund and above all alive. The dream turned nightmare has completed its course, spiraling forth to begin anew.

More shrieks from the pews, and a man stumbles from his seat before fleeing up the aisle. He rushes past the confessionals toward the theatre exit, his mouth covered by both hands. A woman in tears quickly follows, as Maxa continues to rot away onstage. Her face festers, the skin of her hands and fingers webbed with bubbling tissue that molts from her exposed musculature in thick droplets. She lets her dressing gown fall away, and a new outcry resounds from the house at the sight of her tumorous midsection, her belly swollen with distension until it puckers and bursts, the front pew splashed with rancid gore. She smiles at the audience, and a clump of flesh sloughs from her cheek like braised meat.

"Anaïs," Monsieur Guillard murmurs. "Anaïs, you are driving me mad." He gathers me in his lap and turns me toward him, his face between my breasts. "You are the only one for me." How much his words resemble those of Henry! How much they resemble those of Hugo as well, or any number of men threaded through the tapestry of my life. Guillard may well prove a demon, but in essence he is only another man. Only a man, before the fall.

"You claim to answer the darkest prayers of

desperate women," I say, and grasp his shoulders as he bucks beneath me. "Only it is to your own needs that you respond. One would almost think you a real man."

"I am greater than any man," he grunts. "Greater than any being you have ever known."

"You are demonic in nature. Indeed, you are quite powerful. Yet it is unfortunate that you can never feel true pleasure, not fully. Because pleasure belongs only to the realm of the living, and you cannot live as man lives."

"Oh, but I can," Guillard insists with a lustful snarl. "I do as I wish. I am able to make my blood run as hot as any man's blood. I was once a man myself, and I can take you as one just as readily."

"Show me then," I say. "Show me, and we shall find out together, finally and at last. Fill me with your white blood, and take of my flesh. The way only the animal called man can take."

I feel him warming inside me, the chill of his muscle and bone abating. I breathe him in, his ocean scent shifting toward that of the earth, of land and the living. He has become a man again, like any another. And it shall be his undoing.

"I am what my father made me," he says, and he drives deeper inside me, with such force that I bite my lip and draw blood. "As you are yourself."

A flash of movement outside the partition, as June approaches the confessional from her place at the rear of the theater. Despite his sensual reverie, Guillard is quick to take notice of my attention, and he leans forward to peer through the screen.

"Even now as I possess you, you have eyes for another?" he whispers. I expect him to be enraged, but a wicked smile forms upon his lips. "Your affection for her, it radiates from you like light from the sun. All heat. She is delectable indeed."

"She is but another woman," I say, and place my lips close to his ear. "With the same longings and desires and passions that drew you to me. The qualities that drew you to Maxa as well, to all of us. Only you will never have her obedience. You will never possess her as lord and master. And you will never have any part of her, either here in the waking world or in your land of dreams."

"You underestimate me." Guillard grasps the back of my head, his fingers digging into my scalp as he bends forward again to search out a glimpse of June, who has retreated once more. He possesses me, while he thinks of her. "I can take of whomever I please, at the time and place of my choosing."

"Once, perhaps." I reach behind me and remove Sonia's ivory comb from where it tangles in my hair. "But not anymore."

I snap open the comb, raise it up, and plunge the blade into Monsieur Guillard's exposed neck. He heaves, blood exploding from his lips to splash my face as his hands move to stanch his wound, where my weapon found its mark.

"My father made me, it is true," I say, and I raise the blade once more. Beyond the confessional walls, the crowd roars in disgust, shocked exclamations of perverse appreciation echoing across the rows. The cries are intended for Maxa, yet they sustain me. "But I have long since remade myself."

I strike again, against the heavy hand shielding his face. An arc of blood whips free, and Guillard thrusts me away as he staggers to the confessional door. I spring up like a jungle cat and pounce on Guillard's back. Another swing of the deadly comb, and this time I embed it deep between his shoulders. He stumbles against me, his hands moving to strangle me before returning to his own savaged neck.

"What…have you done to me?" he gurgles, blood bubbling at the corner of his mouth.

"I have freed you from your earthly obligations, you accursed fiend. Now, you may rest at last."

He wrests free and hurls himself against the door. Once, twice, and the door bursts wide, the wood splintered as he lurches bleeding from the confessional. The screams outside are louder now, and I scramble half-naked from the box, my dress bunched around my waist and my face and breasts spattered with blood. I grasp his coattails to slow his progress as he stumbles up the aisle toward the exit.

"June! June, help me!" I cry above the raucous audience. She materializes from her nearby post and throws herself in his path to prevent escape. Startled, he retreats down the aisle, and June and I seize his arms, dark blood pooling on the carpet beneath our feet.

A man seated on the aisle stares up at us in confusion. He studies the blade embedded in Guillard's back before his gaze returns to the stage, where Maxa's putrescent form is near collapse. His attention returns to us, however, followed by other audience members, and soon we attract more stares, a dozen theatregoers gaping in our direction as June and I try our best to hold fast to Guillard.

In a matter of a few heartbeats, the entirety of

the Guignol has taken notice. They are unclear of our roles, especially that of the gore-soaked gentleman in our grasp. June glares at me and I look to the stage, to Maxa, who only moments ago had commanded the room as her own. I wipe blood from my face, take a deep breath, and I hold my head up high.

"Hail, Lady Death!" I raise my bloody hand to Maxa in salutation. "Sacred Goddess of the Underworld, we honor you as you undergo your ghastly metamorphosis!"

The audience, mesmerized, turns their attentions back to Maxa. "Now it is your turn," I whisper to June, as Guillard struggles between us. "Go on."

"Hail, Lady Death!" June calls out, and raises her own hand in imitation. "We…We support you in your really disgusting metamorphosis!"

Silence.

"H-hail." Maxa manages to get the word out, black bile spilling from her desiccated lips. "Hail and welcome. S-sisters."

The spotlight trained on Maxa shudders uncertainly before the powerful beam swings in our direction, and we are caught in its unforgiving light. Monsieur Guillard buries his face in his shoulder, but for a brief moment his monstrous visage is made visible, a hideous amalgam of features rendered as if from hot wax poured over cracked stone.

At once, we are shoved forward. The master of ceremonies presses us forward, and we soon find ourselves up the short set of stairs at the foot of the aisle and forced onstage. June, myself, and the expiring Guillard all stand beside Maxa, footlights bathing us in a blood-red glow. We have become a part of the show.

"Accept this sacrifice on behalf of your humble servants," I incant, as loud as my voice will speak. I remember this vantage point well. "And let it be known to all that no man can escape your irrevocable embrace!"

"Accept the sacrifice," June echoes. "And let it be known!"

The demon shrinks in our arms. A dead and dying thing, and even the weight of him seems lessened now. As with all wicked scourges dragged into the light, as with every shameful secret that seeks and fails to remain hidden, his terrible power is at once diminished.

Guillard crumples between us. I tilt my head in the direction of the rear of the theatre, and June helps me drag Guillard's limp body from the stage and back down the aisle. We reach the confessional and thrust him inside, and I scurry after him, June slamming the door behind me. As the audience howls with renewed revulsion and awe at whatever fresh horrors Maxa's flesh has yielded, I drop down to the floor and lower Guillard's head into my lap in a tender pieta.

"How..." he croaks, his life force draining from him, energy depleting as his body begins its own process of mortal decay. "How...can this be possible?"

"Even demons may die, Monsieur Guillard. Indeed, it is the nature of things. In all your vast wanderings and great experience, did you never manage to learn that?"

He stares up and past me, toward the ceiling of the confessional, where his gaze remains eternally fixed. The iron tang of blood commingles with a renewed scent of the roiling ocean, as if I have returned to that rocky shore from the dream. Only now, the demon lover is no more. Now, the storm clouds have parted to let in the light, star shine pricking the heavy blanket of night until all the heavens are aglow.

I stagger to my feet and collapse upon the bench, and stare panting out through the screen, the audience returning their collective scrutiny to the stage. In a jerking motion, Maxa begins to straighten up like a marionette, her fortitude increasing as her body pulls itself erect. Her limbs lengthen and pulse, swaths of corroded skin rippling and stretching over muscle and bone, taut and unblemished until she begins to regain her familiar composition. The patrons gasp with amazement, their cries no longer those of terror, but rather of a holy form of rapture at this holy miracle of resurrection. The monster's demise has brought her back to life.

Restored to a healthful splendor, the likes of which I had yet to see her possess, Maxa lifts her chin to the balcony and strikes a grand pose of triumph. The crowd leaps to their feet and rewards her with a standing ovation that lasts many minutes, long after she bows and leaves the stage. Finally the curtain draws closed, and beneath the renewed glare of the house lights, the applause continues unceasing, theatregoers left stunned and electrified and unsure of just what it is they have seen. The Maddest Woman in the World is whole again, and the chapel of pain and pleasure glows anew.

"Anaïs?" It is June, on the far side of the confessional screen. "Anaïs, is everything okay in there?"

"It is," I say, and I am startled to find that the

words are true. I stare down at the corpse of Monsieur Guillard, the stench of seaweed and brine wafting from his body, as if he is returning from whence he came. "Our terrible problem? I believe it has been solved. Thanks, in part, to you."

I place my palm against the screen. June matches it with hers, our hands separated by the partition but still touching, still connected after all this time.

"What an act, am I right?" Her voice is tremulous, as if she has already begun the process of self-deception that will allow her to bury that which cannot be understood. "I've never seen anything like it! Did you see it, Anaïs?"

"I saw it." An enduring weight lifts, my eyes flooded with tears as a wave of gratitude washes over me, the house lights shining like miniature suns over the sea. A malignant spell has been broken. "It was the performance of a lifetime."

⚭

IT IS ANOTHER month before I work up the courage to return to Allendy's office. I apologize to the doctor for cutting short our last session, and for failing to respond to his many subsequent inquiries after my well-being. "It was a difficult time," I say vaguely, and smooth my dress hem against the edge of the couch. "My life became as a forest in a fairy tale, one I blithely traveled with neither map or compass to guide me. How quickly I became lost, and how fast the darkness descended."

Past midnight, June already departed for her hotel, and Maxa and I endure the harsh bounce of cobblestones as we sit in the back of her actor friend's truck. The space cramped and unlit with the weighty clothes trunk positioned between us, I count the minutes until the truck finally pulls to the curb. We emerge along an esplanade overlooking the Seine, the river swirling in the gloom below. Maxa's friend helps us remove the trunk before he drives away, unwilling to help us any further. Alone beside the Pont Alexandre III, Maxa and I wait unspeaking for the others to arrive.

Soon, we spy Therese and Sonia as they emerge from the other side of the bridge. When they reach us, the four of us nod at one another over the tattered trunk, a grim acknowledgment of our collective survival. With no small amount of difficulty, we carry the heavy trunk down the stone steps to the edge of the riverbank and pause at the bottom so that Therese can paint a crude sigil beside the lock and hasp. "To bind him, even in death," she whispers, as she uses a gnarled finger to ornament the trunk with a viscous white paste that reeks of damp wood and pepper.

The twinkle of lights from distant houseboats, the crisp scent of the river at night, and we heave the trunk over the side. It hits the surface with a loud splash, and we watch it sink beneath the water until it is swallowed altogether. We ascend the stone steps, and it is as if the street lamps upon the esplanade burn with renewed strength. As if all the world is brighter now, at least to those who have endured.

"Fortunately, the clouds seem to have passed." I light a cigarette and fix my gaze on Allendy, challenging him to contradict me. "I feel sure of myself, for the first time in many months, if not years."

"I am happy to hear that. It is obvious, however, that you are still conflicted about treatment. Perhaps your childhood feelings for your father have been projected onto me. It is not difficult to see in our therapeutic relationship a classic representation of transference."

Allendy lights his pipe and chews suggestively at the stem. He suspects unwholesome attractions but not their source, the perverse corruption that exists inside me still. Or perhaps he does know, and is attempting to tease a confession from me. I cannot say for certain.

"Regardless of any conflict," he adds, "it is clear that you are ultimately drawn toward chaos. And toward those who provide it most readily."

"Maybe so. Or perhaps I seek them out in order to end it. To stage a final resolution, one that will grant me a new purpose, a new ability to thrive."

Once Therese and Sonia bid us farewell and depart for the left bank, I plead with Maxa to allow me back to her flat, to help her in breaking her opium habit this very night. She simply shakes her head, and smiles sadly. She delivers to me a gentle kiss, one cheek and the other, and last upon the center of my forehead. Even amid the sorrow of parting, she leaves me feeling anointed.

"Thank you for rescuing me," Maxa says with the innocence of a child, the schoolgirl she was before her own trust was first broken. "I hope you understand that you have managed the impossible. But now we must go our separate ways, and never look back again."

I remain at the entrance of the bridge and watch her leave, in the direction of her flat and the Grand Guignol. Once she is gone, I turn to face the river, and study the surface of the water as it flows past.

I wonder if something finished can ever truly begin again. If that which is dead remains departed, or if new life can spring forth from the old.

"I have weathered the storm," I say to Allendy. "Come out the other side, with a rekindled lust for life. For light and for love, the warmth that only human connection can provide." I draw from my cigarette and exhale forcefully, our smoke commingling in the air. "I have my husband, and my writing as well, and I am dedicated to them both. And yes, I still see Henry. He is there for me, when I am not occupied with Hugo. In that way, they are like my fiction and my diary, two alternate sources of inspiration. My needs are the same as those of many women, and I will follow them as long as I desire."

"And what of June?" Allendy says. "What of your feelings for her?"

Later that night, I visit her shabby hotel room. I sink beneath her dress, June listing as I tug down her underwear and bury myself in her sex. She moans, and I find deeper and deeper destinations, my tongue and lips seeking out every part of her. June grips the edge of the dressing table, her long dancer's legs splayed

ROBERT LEVY

wide to accommodate me, not much time before a new dawn breaks over the Hotel Cronstadt and the whole of Paris awakens from its heavy slumber. Soon, there will be husbands to meet, and old debts to settle, and fantasies to turn away from forever. Not yet, however, because time has no meaning for us. Not here. Not in this endless moment that, delirious with death and sex, we finish between unwashed sheets, my body pressed to hers with Monsieur Guillard's blood still staining our flesh. She becomes mine, and I become hers, in a way that no man can ever undo.

"June is gone," I say, smoke snaking from my lips. "A tour of Italy, and then back to New York, for good this time. According to her own needs as well."

"That is for the best, then. Abnormal pleasures, they…"

"Kill the taste for normal ones?"

"Something of the sort." He taps his pipe into the ashtray. "I believe it would do you good to give the isolation accumulator another go. Step inside the box again, and face your initial resistance. Make a complete circle of it, if you will."

"Doctor, I…" The whistling wind, the sound of the sea rushing in, out, in. Yellow eyes, peering out from the darkness, through the deep. "I do not think that would be wise."

"Come." He gets to his feet and extends a hand toward me. "Let us at least look inside together, shall we? What harm could there be in that?" Reluctantly, I take his hand, and allow him to help me from the couch.

Allendy tells me more about the accumulator's efficacy, how a young doctor at the Vienna Ambulatorium is expanding on the prototype so that the boxes will soon be in the offices of analysts all across Europe, if everything goes as planned. I am not really listening, however. Instead, as he escorts me from the office, I think of this morning, of sitting under the elm in the garden to write in my diary as the bees buzzed through the humid air. Summer arrived early in Louveciennes. Beneath the great tree, I am lost in the act of creation, pages and pages filled with this story I have been so hesitant to tell, for at times it has felt so much like a dream. Yet it is no dream, not any of it. This is the very story of my life.

"Anaïs?" Hugo stands above me with his back to the bright sun, and I squint up at his silhouette, black against the wide blue sky. "I said, I am off to work. Didn't you hear me calling you?"

"I am sorry, my love. I was in another world. But I have returned now." We embrace, and even in this moment I am eager to return to my diary and darken its every page with ink. "Emilia and I will make sure everything is prepared for dinner. All you have to do is return."

"I will be sure to do that. Until then, my darling." We kiss, and when he turns to go, I settle again beneath the elm. "I almost forgot," he says and turns back, his body rendered a shadow once more. "A telegram came for you earlier. It was from your father."

"My father?" My voice trembles, I can barely draw breath. "What is it? Is everything all right?"

"Quite all right, yes. He is finally returning to France. In fact, he plans to be in Paris in a few short weeks. He wants to see us. Wants to see you, that is." Hugo takes the telegram from his pocket and hands it to me. "Won't it be lovely to have him so close, and after all this time?"

"Of course." I force myself to smile up at him. "What a wonderful surprise."

I place the telegram inside my diary, close it up between these brown marbled covers. The way I attempt to trap so many things inside, even with the knowledge that someday it will all come pouring forth, no matter how hard I wish it otherwise. The truth, as they say, will out.

The loud clang of the garden gate as Hugo departs, and I stare back at the house, count the eleven shutters thrown wide until I reach the closed one in the middle. The sealed room, shut tight as ever. I clutch my diary to my chest, and attempt to calm my racing heart, which pounds with fear and apprehension.

Beneath the steady gallop, however, I sense another rhythm. A wilder beat, one that cuts through the air with steel wings, with a wicked and possessed anticipation. I bring my diary to my mouth and press my lips against it, the violent heat of desire overtaking me until I am certain I will be consumed.

Allendy leads me to the parlor, and I step past him and inside. My eyes fall upon the accumulator once more, the imposing wood-slatted box set against the far wall, the door flung wide onto its cold interior. As I slowly approach, I feel its powerful pagan draw, and stand before its open mouth as a naked child stands before the hungry throat of a cave. No powers or magical gifts granted, only my own essential humanity, a woman alone on her solitary journey.

June was correct: it is no longer safe, not anywhere in the world. Especially for women like us. I must choose my path forward wisely.

The creak of a loose floorboard, and Allendy's hot breath brushes against my bare neck, his hands gripping tight to my shoulders. I think of the sealed room, of myself as a little girl, my father as he embraces me from behind. I remember the fear, commingled as it was with fascination, and yes, with a perverse kind of pleasure as well.

I turn, and I face him. I face them all.

ABOUT THE AUTHOR

ROBERT LEVY'S first novel *The Glittering World* was a finalist for the Lambda Literary Award as well as the Shirley Jackson Award, while shorter work has appeared in *Black Static, Shadows & Tall Trees*, and *The Dark*, as well as "Best Of" anthologies *The Best Horror of the Year*, *Wilde Stories: The Year's Best Gay Speculative Fiction*, and *The Year's Best Hardcore Horror*, among others. A Brooklyn native, he teaches at the Stonecoast MFA Program in Creative Writing and can be found online at TheRobertLevy.com.